"I've Been Challenged By My Great-Aunt Hazel To Seduce You," Lyndie Said. "She Doesn't Think I Can Do It, But I Think I Can."

Bruce stared at her in the darkness of the paddock. She couldn't read his expression at all.

"It would delight me to no end to prove her and her wicked matchmaking ways wrong. Would you go along with the gag?"

He stepped toward her, tall and intimidating, masculine and domineering.

"I'll go along with it. How far are we going?"

"Well—not far enough for me to be a notch on your bedpost," she confirmed nervously.

"I'd rather you be tethered to my bedpost." He pressed his long, lean body against hers.

She looked up at him, wondering how feminine wiles could ever tame such a male animal. Against her will, her breath quickened. She was no match for him when his very nearness caused her to tremble and melt.

"This is just to fool Hazel," she said. "I'm not really going to try to seduce you. You do understand that, don't you?"

He nodded.

Then, in a harsh whisper, he said, "I know. 'Cause *I'm* going to seduce *you*...."

Dear Reader,

In honor of International Women's Day, March 8, celebrate romance, love and the accomplishments of women all over the world by reading six passionate, powerful and provocative new titles from Silhouette Desire.

New York Times bestselling author Sharon Sala leads the Desire lineup with *Amber by Night* (#1495). A shy librarian uses her alter ego to win her lover's heart in a sizzling love story by this beloved MIRA and Intimate Moments author. Next, a pretend affair turns to true passion when a Barone heroine takes on the competition, in *Sleeping with Her Rival* (#1496) by Sheri WhiteFeather, the third title of the compelling DYNASTIES: THE BARONES saga.

A single mom shares a heated kiss with a stranger on New Year's Eve and soon after reencounters him at work, in *Renegade Millionaire* (1497) by Kristi Gold. *Mail-Order Prince in Her Bed* (#1498) by Kathryn Jensen features an Italian nobleman who teaches an American ingenue the language of love, while a city girl and a rancher get together with the help of her elderly aunt, in *The Cowboy Claims His Lady* (#1499) by Meagan McKinney, the latest MATCHED IN MONTANA title. And a contractor searching for his secret son finds love in the arms of the boy's adoptive mother, in *Tangled Sheets, Tangled Lies* (#1500) by brand-new author Julie Hogan, debuting in the Desire line.

Delight in all six of these sexy Silhouette Desire titles this month…and every month.

Enjoy!

Joan Marlow Golan

Joan Marlow Golan
Senior Editor, Silhouette Desire

The Cowboy Claims His Lady

MEGAN McKINNEY

Silhouette® Desire®

Published by Silhouette Books

America's Publisher of Contemporary Romance

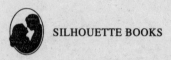

SILHOUETTE BOOKS

ISBN 0-373-76499-5

THE COWBOY CLAIMS HIS LADY

Visit Silhouette at www.eHarlequin.com

Printed in U.S.A.

Books by Meagan McKinney

Silhouette Desire

One Small Secret #1222
*The Cowboy Meets His Match #1299
*The M.D. Courts His Nurse #1354
*Plain Jane & the Hotshot #1493
*The Cowboy Claims His Lady #1499

Silhouette Intimate Moments

*The Lawman Meets His Bride #1037

*Matched in Montana

MEAGAN McKINNEY

is the author of over a dozen hardcover and paperback historical and contemporary women's fiction novels. In addition to romance, she likes to inject mystery and thriller elements into her work. Currently she lives in the Garden District of New Orleans with her two young sons, two very self-entitled cats and a crazy red mutt. Her favorite hobbies are traveling to the Arctic and, of course, reading!

One

"**G**et over here and give this old cowgirl a hug!"

Melynda Clay laughed at the greeting. She heard the familiar voice before she could even glance across the small airport terminal of Mystery, Montana.

"Hazel!"

Tugging her wheeled luggage behind her, Lyndie headed toward the petite older woman with the elegant silver-chignoned hair. Her great-aunt was the same old contradiction in terms Lyndie remembered. The handsome cattle baroness also wore faded jeans tucked into dusty cowboy boots and a smart alligator-band Western hat.

"So how is my notorious great-aunt?" Lyndie asked with laughter and a hug.

"Right as rain on a wood duck! Never better!"

Lyndie had to agree. Hazel McCallum didn't look a day over sixty but the matriarch was well into the next decade.

All that clean-living and fresh mountain air, Lyndie mused. Certainly it was the opposite of the life she'd been living recently, bent over accounting books, worrying and biting her nails in the back of her little French Quarter shop in New Orleans.

"Lands, let me look at you!" Hazel exclaimed, holding Lyndie out at arm's length. "Hon, I love what you've done with your hair. Last time I saw you, you were just graduating college and you practically had a buzz cut, remember?"

"Remember? Are you kidding? You kept asking me if I'd joined the Marines!"

"Well, the shoulder length and the blond streaks are perfect for your McCallum good looks," Hazel said approvingly, still admiring her. "You've got my daddy's sapphire-blue eyes. My gosh, you're a regular traffic hazard."

Hazel narrowed her own Prussian-blue eyes as if seeing more than Lyndie wanted her to. Lyndie wondered if her great-aunt was taking note of the signs of chronic strain and worry molding her features these days, especially the dark circles under those "sapphire-blue eyes." The smudges betrayed the days of endless fretting and the sleepless nights.

"Well, c'mon, city slicker," Hazel said, taking Lyndie's free hand and pulling her toward the parking lot. "I'm parked right out front. You'll find no chauffeur-driven Jaguars around here. Just my dusty old Caddy with tumbleweeds stuck in the grill and longhorns for a hood ornament."

"Chauffeur-driven Jaguars?" Lyndie repeated, gasping. "Aunt Hazel, I'm not doing *that* well."

"Oh, cowplop! Your mom tells me you're getting ready to open your second store. That lingerie empire of yours is practically now a conglomerate. I'm proud of you, sweetie. I guess there's two sharp business tycoons in this family. So don't you let those cowhands of mine tease you mercilessly about those underwear shops."

"'All for Milady,'" Lyndie replied, hamming it up for her favorite relative and quoting from the advertising copy Lyndie had written herself, "'offers a complete line of women's intimate apparel, the latest in fit and luxury for the discriminating woman.'"

Hazel rolled her eyes. "Oh, brother! Intimate apparel? All my cowboys know about a 'teddy' is that he was once the president."

They emerged into the sun-drenched late afternoon, a gorgeous June day. Lyndie was amazed that Hazel had meant it literally when she said she was parked right out front. Her cinnamon-and-black Fleetwood sat only about ten feet from the front doors. The small parking lot was almost empty.

"The only reason they call this paved pasture an airport," Hazel informed her niece as they stored her luggage in the trunk, "is that we get a few flights from Helena. You're in back of beyond now, girl. And I still say it's just what you need. Your mom Sarah's been telling me you've been working from get-up to go-to-bed, seven days a week."

Lyndie managed a woeful smile. "I'm glad to be out west, Aunt Hazel, and to see you. But I confess I'm not so sure about this dude ranch of yours. That part is a little off-kilter right now."

"Land sakes, why?"

"Oh, you know…I'm not really in the mood to be bonding with a bunch of tourists—"

"Oh, pouf! Besides, Bruce will keep all of you so dang busy there won't be much time for idle jaw-boning."

"Bruce?"

"You remember, I mentioned him to you on the phone? He trains and breeds horses for all us ranchers in Mystery Valley. During the summer he also runs Mystery Dude, from May to September. With some help, of course."

Lyndie could have sworn she saw a glint of shrewdness in Hazel's eyes as she added, "He's also one of the most eligible hunks in the valley. 'Bedroom eyes' as us older gals used to say. He puts me in mind of Gregory Peck in his salad days."

"Oh, no you don't!"

Hazel glanced over, the very picture of faux shock. "Oh, no I don't—what?"

"Aunt Hazel, I know good and well a scheming mind lurks behind that innocent-little-old-lady exterior of yours. I told you I wouldn't come if I was to be one of your victims. Mom has told me all about your little matchmaking schemes, and I made it clear I'll take no part in—"

"Schemes?" Hazel protested. "I've...facilitated a romance or two, perhaps, but—"

"Four weddings in one year? Mom says you even use notches now to count them."

"Oh, you know Sarah," Hazel said dismissively, "that niece of mine always liked to stretch the blanket a mite."

"Uh-huh, sure. Well, please don't try to 'facilitate' anything for me, okay? A little fun and diversion, well, all right, I'll give that a whirl. But believe me, right now 'romance' is the last thing I need."

"Now, you needn't be so testy," Hazel scolded. "I simply remarked that Bruce is good-looking, and here you go and erupt like Mount Vesuvius."

"I'm sorry." Lyndie sighed, wondering if she had been overreacting. She was certainly prone to it these days.

Hazel nattered on enthusiastically about Mystery

Dude Ranch while Lyndie dutifully tried to pay attention. Outside, the brittle light of late afternoon was taking on the mellow richness of sunset. White gauze clouds drifted in a deep cerulean sky, with majestic mountains forming a postcard-perfect Western vista. Mystery, Montana, was downright sublime in its natural beauty.

Lyndie abruptly realized Hazel had asked her a question.

"I'm sorry, what'd you say, Aunt Hazel?"

"I said, Mystery Dude is right on the way to my place. Since you'll be moving in there tomorrow, anyway, why don't we swing by and leave your cowpoke duds in your room? It's close to supper, Bruce should be back to the house now. You can meet him."

Lyndie aimed a suspicious glance at her.

"No Cupid tricks," Hazel assured her. "Honest. Just to give you the lay of the land, that's all."

"Sure," Lyndie responded, perking up a bit. "You're right. That way we won't have to haul my stuff around needlessly."

A grin divided Hazel's weather-seamed face. "Now you're whistlin'! Maybe we can even pick out your horse."

Lyndie could have sworn the sly glint was back in Hazel's eyes when she added, "If there's one thing Bruce Everett is a good judge of, it's horseflesh."

* * *

As if the place were only remembered in dreams, Lyndie realized she had forgotten how breathtaking Mystery Valley was—a patchwork of verdant pastures and fields like spokes radiating from the hub of the town of Mystery, population four thousand. About ten minutes after they entered the valley through a winding mountain pass, Hazel swung the Fleetwood off onto a dirt lane. The lane led to a ranch much smaller than her own Lazy M that dominated the valley.

"Why, there's Bruce now," Hazel remarked, tooting the horn as she pulled up in front of a long stone watering trough.

Perhaps a dozen or so people of both sexes and various ages, most with Lyndie's unmistakable look of "city slickers," stood near a big pole corral watching something—or someone. The car rolled a few more feet forward, and then Lyndie spotted a tall, lean, weather-bronzed man who was evidently demonstrating how to cinch a girth, using a barrel-chested sorrel horse as his model.

"This is the second new group of the season," Hazel explained as both women got out of the car. "Bruce takes a new group every three weeks—that way everybody's on the same page."

Bruce Everett smiled and waved a greeting at Hazel, excusing himself from the group and striding over to meet the new arrivals.

Even from where she was, Lyndie could see he was indeed handsome, but she felt an almost physical backlash to her attraction, and she couldn't help but think of the old truism "Once burned, twice shy."

"Hazel, you cattle rustler!" he called out cheerfully. "What have you come to swindle me out of now?"

"*Me* the swindler! You're the one who sells spavined horses to unsuspecting old ladies."

During this exchange of fond insults, his gaze quickly appraised Lyndie. For some reason, Hazel's comment about his prowess in judging horseflesh just wouldn't leave Lyndie's mind.

"Bruce Everett," Hazel announced, handling the introductions, "this is my grand-niece from New Orleans, Melynda Clay. But everybody calls her Lyndie. She doesn't know beans about horses, but I expect you to remedy that in the next few weeks."

"As long as she's sound of limb and wind," he assured Hazel, "we can turn her into a cowgirl. Glad to meetcha, Lyndie."

His strong white teeth flashed in a wolfish smile, and an eerie, unpleasant sense of déjà vu washed over her. There was a confidence—a confidence bordering on arrogance—about this man that was reminiscent of Lyndie's ex-husband Mitch's manner. But whereas Mitch was all show and no substance, something told Lyndie to be wary of this cowboy's confidence. It just might turn out to be the real thing.

His scrutiny trapped her.

Suddenly irritated, she flung him a frozen, perfunctory smile, then let her gaze turn to study a group of horses in a paddock beside the sprawling stone ranch house. As she'd hoped, her dismissal of him was obvious.

"Same here," she intoned in a pleasant, detached manner, her attention glued to the paddock.

"Well, that gets *my* money," she thought she heard him say under his breath.

Hazel raised her voice for Lyndie's benefit and suggested cheerfully, "Bruce, maybe you two could pick out Lyndie's horse while she's here."

They joined her near the paddock.

"That little bay mare with the white socks is one of my favorites," he told Lyndie. "'Course, they're all good animals. They're not what you'd call well-schooled in dressage, but all of them are honest and fit. They do to take along."

Lyndie chanced a longer look at him this time.

He had removed his hat, and a shock of jet-black hair curved across his strong brow. The eyes watching her were the shade of morning frost.

He didn't have Mitch's features, no. But the handsome smile and the confidence—they were reminiscent of the traits she had fallen for hardest in Mitch. And the very thought of him still soured her blood.

"They'll do to take along where?" she replied, though she knew full well it was just a westernism he had spoken, not a literal remark.

He gave another interrogative glance at Hazel. "Wherever I take 'em," he replied, placing slight emphasis on the word *I*.

Hazel, her expression clearly betraying how much she did not like the trail they were taking, again spoke up.

"You know, hon, I just remembered you must be tired from your trip. You can pick out your horse tomorrow. Why don't we just take a quick look at your room, then head on to the Lazy M?"

"That's sound just like the tonic I need," Lyndie said.

Bruce seemed to want to elaborate on what kind of tonic he'd like to give her, but to his credit, he directed "Right this way," leading them toward a low building of new milled lumber that stood between the main house and a row of stables.

"This here's the bunkhouse." He threw open a door. "The place has been renovated to make private rooms. As you see, they're basic, but they're clean as the bottom of a feed bucket. And there's plenty of hot water."

Lyndie stepped into the room. Her black Italian pantsuit looked absolutely out of place next to the rough-hewn log bed and the throw rug covering the floor. She already felt like a fish out of water, and only more so when she turned and met the cowboy's gyrfalcon gaze.

There was no reading his mind. He was like Mitch, a cipher. But she swore she saw the twist of a smirk on his lips as he, too, noticed the contrast between her and the simple room.

Rattled, she ran her hand down the thick, scratchy wool blanket on the bed. "Well, I didn't expect the Ritz, so I guess this will serve its purpose just fine," she said dismissively.

His gray eyes lit with an amused sparkle. "It's always served my purposes damn well—"

Hazel interrupted him with a coughing fit. "Lordy, don't know what came over me," she apologized when she was finished.

"I—I guess I'll get my bag, then," Lyndie remarked.

"Let me help you," he offered.

"Thanks, I can manage," she assured him, walking out the door without turning around.

He stared at her until she turned the corner.

"Well, ain't *she* silky satin," he mumbled under his breath.

Hazel grinned. "Actually, she is."

He raised one dark eyebrow.

"She's in the lingerie business, remember?"

He grinned back. "That's right. Well, either she's got a mighty high opinion of herself, or a mighty low opinion of everyone else."

"Neither one," Hazel insisted. "She's a wonderful girl. Just give her a little time, that's all."

Bruce lifted the corner of his mouth in a smirking smile. The gray of his eyes deepened. "Tell you what, Hazel, her nose may be a little out of joint, but the rest of her sure seems to be in order."

"Atta boy," Hazel encouraged him. "You just keep thinking like that, and sooner or later things are going to start humming right along."

He narrowed his eyes in suspicion. "Humming along? Hey, I just run a dude ranch here, Hazel, and I try to be civil with all comers. I got no ulterior motives regarding your niece."

"Well, you'd better get some," Hazel insisted.

His jaw slackened in surprise.

But before he could respond, Hazel said, "Shush now, here she comes."

"The hell you up to now, old gal?" he muttered.

"Just the usual tricks," she muttered right back, quelling her smile before Lyndie saw it. "Just the usual tricks."

TWO

Bumping her wheeled suitcase along the dirt road toward the bunkhouse, Lyndie began to wonder what she'd gotten into.

A couple of weeks at a dude ranch had sounded fine in the steaming French Quarter—but that was then. Now she found herself in her high-heeled designer shoes, having to negotiate a hoof-rutted dirt path—not to mention the treacherous road map of a certain Mr. Everett.

He'd shaken her more than she wanted to admit. The lazy, hooded stare sparked something inside her which she feared was lust.

But she was not going down that highway to hell.

Not now. Not ever. Fancy lingerie was fine for married women and the swinging single gal, but she was a businesswoman, and the lacy, sheer demi-bras she sold were now nothing more to her than product. They were the accoutrements of some other world, not of her own.

"Ma'am," a deep-chested voice said in her ear.

Somehow he'd appeared beside her. She faced the ice-gray eyes of Bruce Everett.

He took her suitcase and hefted it easily to his shoulder like a favorite saddle.

"That's all right—no—really, I can manage—" she stammered, following him like a schoolgirl.

"Been told you can manage just about anything—given what Hazel says about you," he answered gruffly.

He turned and they locked stares.

Again she was frozen by his gaze.

Hazel showed up at the bunkhouse door, beaming. "We've got a good, old-fashioned Saturday night stomp at the Mystery Saloon tonight. You thinkin' of comin', Bruce?"

Lyndie cringed. She suddenly felt like she was in junior high, waiting for that first guy to ask her to dance. And there were no takers.

"You know I go for the trail and not the saloon, Hazel," he answered gruffly.

Her great-aunt snorted like she was one of the cowpokes. "There was a time before Katherine that you were all too familiar with the saloon, and it's time you stepped out again.''

If Lyndie didn't know better, she would have sworn Bruce Everett gave Hazel one of those perma-frost looks she was beginning to recognize herself. But that was not possible. No one thwarted Hazel. Hazel was the grand-dame of Mystery, Montana.

The McCallums went back more than a century, and had settled the entire valley. Among cattle ranchers, the McCallum name was interchangeable with the Midas touch. Even Lyndie herself knew how persuasive her great-aunt could be. In the midst of expansion and fiscal crisis, Lyndie had been lured to drop everything and attend a three-week vacation at a dude ranch—when she didn't even know how to ride.

"We'll see you at the stomp," Hazel announced.

Bruce stood and stared at the two women, Lyn-die's leaden suitcase still perched on his broad shoulder.

"Well, if looks could kill..." Lyndie murmured as soon as she was locked inside Hazel's signature burnt-orange Caddy and away from the eyes and ears of Bruce Everett.

"He just needs a nudge, that's all."

She looked at her great-aunt. "Hazel, I said no shenanigans. I certainly don't need them, not when you've convinced me to take a break. And certainly

Bruce Everett doesn't need a woman thrown in his lap when he has this Katherine he's hung up on.''

"He needs to quit his hang-up with Katherine. It wasn't his fault. She was a headstrong fool who couldn't be taught to respect a horse. And I don't care how beautiful she was, he had no business with a woman who wouldn't respect a horse," Hazel said astutely.

"I am totally confused. What does this have to do with me?" Lyndie enquired. "Because, let me tell you, I respect horses. In fact, if the truth be known, I so respect them that I'm scared to death of them. So let Bruce and Katherine have their respect-the-horse love-fest without me.''

"He needs to go to the saloon tonight and two-step around a bit. It'd be good for what ails him. There was a time when he was the tomcat of Mystery. And believe me, the ladies didn't complain.''

Lyndie released a cynical sigh. "I know too well of what you speak, Hazel, but his tomcat ways sound like Katherine's problem.''

"Katherine's dead.''

Lyndie gave her a sharp look.

"Yep," Hazel continued. "She died on the trail with Bruce. There was talk he was in love with her. There was even rumor of a wedding. But Katherine had no horse sense, literally. She felt horses were no better than men, ready to serve her beck and call. When the bobcat attacked, she didn't realize the cat was protecting her litter. Katherine ignored all her mount's warnings, and, in my opinion, that's why she was bucked and fell to her death off that cliff.''

The news punched Lyndie in the gut. Empathy, something she swore she'd feel for no man after Mitch, came swelling up inside her. "I had no idea," she said softly. "Gosh, how awful for him."

"Yep. And him the kind of man who likes to have everything in control," Hazel said solemnly.

"Maybe you ought to leave him alone, Hazel. After all, I'm sure he feels guilty—"

"Guilty? Why should he feel guilty? It wasn't his fault. The horse neighed and shied. And then shied and shied again. She shouldn't have forced the poor animal. But that Katherine, she was the kind of gal who never took 'no' for an answer, and she spurred that poor frightened animal to its death. Along with hers."

"How horrible." A sympathetic moan emanated from Lyndie's lips. "No wonder he's so cold."

"He was never cold before. But now he punishes himself every day."

"Terrible."

Hazel took a deep breath as she sped the Caddy along the dusty gravel roads toward her ranch. Every now and again, the matron gave Lyndie a probing glance. "It's not your concern whether Bruce Everett heals or not. It's just that the man works so hard. It's as if he's running from something—and I just want to see him stop and turn around, is all. Success is useless if you can't have some fun now and then.''

Lyndie grew pensive, thinking of her own situation. Her divorce had been public and humiliating, but even worse was the inexpressible shock of betrayal, the sudden discovery that her ''charming and loving'' husband had been not only embezzling money from her for years, but using the funds to support his mistress.

Swindling his wife, betraying his wedding vows and her trust—it had meant no more to Mitch than killing a fly.

Suddenly, wanting to confide in Hazel, she said, ''You know, Hazel, I didn't always work like a slave. I used to have fun, but…well, the fun in me just ran out, I guess. I kind of understand where Bruce Everett's coming from. Lately, work's been my only antidote, you know? Sometimes I think that after going through a divorce, 'hell' is a redundant concept.''

Hazel gave her another study, then soothed, ''You just have to let it go, hon, you hear me? What's done is done, and it can't be changed now. Remember, people come out west to start all over. From now on you have to be forward-oriented. And a few weeks at the Mystery Dude Ranch is just what you need.''

Despite the breathtaking summer panorama, Lyn-

die still felt a chill settle on her as she remembered
a much different, much uglier picture from last fall
in New Orleans. She had returned home unexpectedly early from a business trip to Manhattan. Nothing in her life could have prepared her for the shock
of opening the front door and seeing the man she
loved, naked and in the throes of orgasmic bliss with
a woman she had never even suspected existed.

She had tried so hard, in the difficult, intervening
months, to erase that picture, to somehow focus on
the good in her life and expunge the bad. But her
own mother's divorce had left permanent scars.
Somehow work seemed the only way to heal. At
least she wouldn't be impoverished as her mother
had been when Dad had kissed them all off for a
younger woman. Her mother had been abandoned,
with no skills, and no job, and a young child of five
to raise all by herself. Work was a way to restore
her pride, as her mother's pride had been restored
when she went back to school and refused to let the
McCallum money raise her child.

But no matter how hard Lyndie tried, it seemed
that negative thoughts always had the upper hand;
already the "good times" she had shared with Mitch
had become a formless mist in her memory, while
the sharply defined edges of the ugliness still rubbed
her raw....

You have *to curb such thinking,* Lyndie lectured
herself, *or the entire trip will be a waste.*

"I said, has success tied your tongue? Lands, when you were little, everybody called you Babbling Brook, you rambled on so."

The memory coaxed a little one-sided smile out of Lyndie. "I forgot about that name."

Despite the brave front, Lyndie felt the old familiar sting of unshed tears. Even as Hazel watched, Lyndie temporarily lost the battle and one lone tear tipped from her lower lid.

"Love," Hazel said gently, "they say the best way to cure a boil is to lance it. If you want to talk about something, anything, you just get it off your chest, you hear me? I'm a crusty old dame, it's true, but I'm an excellent listener."

"Oh, I'm fine," Lyndie demurred, angrily swiping at the proof she was fibbing. "And I'm sorry for the sob stuff. I honestly didn't come out here to be gloomy and weepy."

"Save your embarrassed apologies for somebody who doesn't love you. You just need to get busy is all. But don't you think I'm doing one of those silly fix-ups with Bruce Everett. That's not it. He's my own special project. I just want to bring out the tomcat in him again. And being a woman of a certain age, I know I can't do it all myself, so I'll have to see if the gals at the stomp can do him some good."

Lyndie couldn't suppress her smile. "Since when do you eliminate yourself on account of age?"

Hazel grinned. "All right. I may be old, but I'm

not dead. And that Bruce Everett is a piece of sirloin that'd be a shame to go to waste.''

Lyndie shrugged. ''I guess it's a pity I'm vegetarian, then.''

''So far,'' Hazel bested, then pressed down the accelerator.

Hazel's guest room was as posh as that in any five-star hotel, but one that blessedly lacked pretension. Curling her toes in the thick Tabriz carpet, Lyndie studied herself in the hand-hewn pine mirror and wondered if she would pass as a Montana native.

She wore her great-aunt's cowboy boots, the ones Hazel wore every day and which possessed enough scrapes and mud to prove it. Tugging on jeans and a simple white cotton T-shirt, she thought the transformation complete, until Hazel knocked on the door and handed her a black cowgirl hat and a pair of dangling turquoise earrings.

''Now you're fit to stomp,'' Hazel pronounced, tipping her own custom-made Stetson.

''Then, too bad Mitch isn't here,'' Lyndie mumbled on the way to the Caddy. ''Cause I'd sure like to stomp him.''

The dance was held at the old Mystery Saloon, circa nineteen-ten. There was a line to get in at the door, but the minute the Caddy pulled up, a skinny young man in a white cowboy hat opened the door for Hazel, and after helping the cattle baroness to her feet, he immediately went to park the car.

"You're certainly the celebrity," Lyndie marveled as the crowd parted to let them in first.

"When you're older than God, the young folks humor you," Hazel quipped, winking at her.

Lyndie gave her a wry smile and said, "Ri-i-i-ight."

The western band was already up and running with a two-step. The room was alive with couples having a good time, and Lyndie suddenly felt her aloneness. To get her mind off the negative, she played tourist. She studied the exquisite truss-work of spruce that held the roof, and she was most impressed by the oak dance floor, worn to an ice-pond finish by nearly a century of sliding cowboy boots.

"When in Rome," Hazel said, handing her a glass from the bartender.

Lyndie took a sip and coughed. "This is whiskey!"

"Like I said, dear, 'When in Rome,'" Hazel repeated, smiling secretively.

"I'm not much of a drinker..." Lyndie tried another sip. The next one didn't burn nearly as much.

"That which doesn't kill you, my dear..."

"Yeah, I know. But I'm really sick of having to be so strong."

Hazel gave her another one of those tricky smiles. "That's what tonight is for. Don't be strong tonight.

Just loosen that girth a little and— Why, speak of the devil! There's Bruce Everett!''

Lyndie looked across the packed dance floor.

She found him in the haze, leaning against the bar like a gunslinger. She'd thought he was tall, but in the crowd he looked even taller, gazing over the crowd with those shuttered, unapproachable eyes.

"Look! He's seen us! He's coming over!" Hazel exclaimed with glee.

Suddenly the whiskey started tasting pretty good to Lyndie. Another gulp and she was prepared to meet those silvery eyes.

"Miss Clay, Hazel," he said, tugging on the front of his black cowboy hat.

"Why aren't you out there on the floor boot-scootin'?" Hazel demanded.

"I was waiting for you," he offered, taking Hazel's arm and wrapping it inside his, as he led her away.

Lyndie watched the two on the dance floor. Bruce and Hazel waltzed as if they'd been made for each other. As they floated and laughed around the crowded floor, Lyndie gripped her whiskey. She was feeling braver, and yet more out of her element with every passing second.

And for this, she had agreed to a vacation?

She should have stayed home. It was less bruising to her ego to spend every day hunched over her books, than hunched over a bar, hoping some cow-poke would ask her to dance.

Bruce brought Hazel back to the hitching post that separated the bar from the dance floor. Lyndie leaned against it, anticipating the moment he'd ask her. She couldn't dance a two-step but she was suddenly eager to try.

She watched as Bruce whispered something in Hazel's ear.

The cattle baroness laughed.

Then he was gone, like a shadowy sharpshooter who dissipated in the mist.

"Well, I'll be," Lyndie muttered.

"You'll be what, dear?" Hazel asked.

"Oh, nothing."

Hazel winked at Lyndie's empty whiskey glass. "Why, you've gone dry!" She was off to the bar before Lyndie could stop her.

It was another hour before she saw Bruce Everett again. Lyndie spied with him a young brunette who was falling all over him on the dance floor.

"Don't you think he's robbing the cradle a bit there?" she muttered over her glass.

"Who?"

Lyndie went to point out Bruce, but the waltz had stopped and the band picked up a lively two-step.

"Dance?"

She looked up and found Bruce next to her, his dark expression quizzical.

It took a moment for Lyndie to realize what Hazel had done. The cattle baroness had to have known that after watching all the couples dancing for an hour, and downing a couple of stiff ones, Lyndie would be tipsy and, at last, ever so grateful to be asked to dance.

"Just because you're paranoid doesn't mean they're *not* out to get you," she joked to herself before taking Bruce's strong arm.

Out on the dance floor she had some difficulty following him. Then suddenly she burst out, "I get it! A two-step is really three steps!"

He laughed. His teeth were very white.

The vision sent an unwanted thrill down her back.

"Give the little lady a hand," he smirked, pulling her back into sync with him.

"This is fun, actually," she confessed.

"'Course it is. Why else would we do it, then?"

She looked up at him, capturing his gaze through the shadow of his low-slung hat.

"I'd better watch out," she teased. "A girl could get used to having fun and not working so hard."

"Why do you need to work so hard? I thought you were the boss."

"That's exactly why I have to work so hard. I'm expanding and I can't find a silent partner, so I'm having the worst time financing—"

She giggled and put her hand to her mouth. "I'm sorry. I don't want to bore you."

"You're not boring me," he said, his gaze never leaving her.

She laughed out loud. "But it's technical. You won't understand."

"I may not be an MBA from one of those fancy East Coast schools, but I understand a good—"

She put her hand to his mouth. His lips were taut with suppressed anger, and she wondered what it would be like to try to kiss the anger away.

"Look, I don't want to ruffle your feathers. I'm here on a vacation. To have fun. So let's have fun."

He pulled her around the dance floor one more time before he spoke.

"You wanna have fun?" He seemed like he'd pondered something for a while and finally had made up his mind.

"Sure," she said lightly.

"Have you seen the old gristmill?"

"I don't think I've ever seen an old gristmill— let alone the one here in Mystery."

"Then, let's go." He stopped dancing and took her hand.

The whiskey must have really hit her hard because she heard herself saying, "What do you do at the mill?" instead of, "My God, I'm not going anywhere with you *alone!*"

"Skinny-dip," he answered.

She took this bit of news more calmly than she

would have expected. "But you don't understand. I can't—" she began.

He stopped her. "Sure you can. Just take off your clothes and jump in. It's easy."

"Take off my clothes?" she repeated numbly. "I really don't think I can take off my—"

"Hey, you're the underwear queen. I thought showing off the merchandise would be second nature." he countered.

"Just 'cause I sell lingerie doesn't mean I can go around—"

"Sure it does," he said soothingly, putting a vise-like grip on her arm as he led her away.

"No really," she countered, but still let him lead her.

"I'll make you a deal then. I'll let you keep on everything you sell in your shop."

"It'll just bore you. I only wear what's beige and functional. I save the froufrou for the customers."

He seemed to hold back a grin. "I'm a cowboy, ma'am. Plain and simple's just fine with me. In fact, you'd like to get plain right down to your birthday suit—"

"I couldn't. I just couldn't," she added.

He grinned in full. "Then, bore me with the beige and functional. And hey, think of it as advertising. Do it for the business. It's good customer relations to show off the merchandise."

She didn't really have an answer for that one.

His arm went around her waist and soon they were out the door.

"Shouldn't I have told Hazel where I'll be?" she asked before getting into an old faded-red pickup.

"You never lived in a small town, did you?" he asked, sliding behind the steering wheel.

"Nope," she answered with more vigor than was necessary.

"Believe me, everybody, including Hazel, knows we're going to the mill."

"Now, how can that be?" she murmured stumped. "Does everybody here have cell phones I can't see?"

"Don't need 'em. We've got Hazel McCallum—and everyone reports to Hazel the goings on 'round here. That's twice true if it concerns one of her own."

He smiled that carnivore's smile and said, "So are you ready?"

She looked at him in the dark. Suddenly she wanted to get out and run.

"I guess," she whispered, all the while wondering what madness had gotten hold of her.

"I'm only doing this because Hazel trusts you. Otherwise, let me tell you, I never go off with strangers." Lyndie rambled on while the pickup negotiated the unpaved mountain road.

"I'm no stranger," Bruce said. "Ask Hazel."

"She says you used to be a tomcat. And even this city girl can figure out what that means."

"Haven't been tomcatting in a while," he almost whispered.

"She told me that, too."

A silence permeated the truck's cab. It was so deep and oppressive, Lyndie was glad when the silhouette of the mill appeared over the hill.

"Here we are."

He pulled next to the fieldstone building. A small river emptied alongside the building and drove the wheel. Beneath it all was a large inviting pool of river water that shimmered in the opalescent moonlight.

She opened her door and got out.

The creaking wheel and the splash of water suddenly set her nerves on edge. As did the tall dark man next to her.

"So, what do you do here?" she asked in a tough voice.

"Swim. I'll show you."

He tugged his shirt out of his jeans and peeled it over his head.

In the moonlight, she could see the ripple of muscle on his chest. There was also a light sprinkling of dark hair that narrowed where his abdominal muscles tightened into a grid. It formed a trail that disappeared into the waist of his jeans.

When he reached for the button on his jeans, she held up her hand.

"If I'm giving a lingerie show, then, so are you. Keep 'em on," she instructed, gesturing to his white boxers that showed through his fly.

"You sure you've never done this before?" He grinned.

She nodded. "I'm sure."

Tossing off his hat and scuffing out of his boots, he finally stood in his boxers, arms crossed as if impatiently waiting for her to follow suit.

A lump of anxiety caught in her throat, but the whiskey told her she wasn't out of her mind—that it was perfectly acceptable to go swimming with a man she'd only met that afternoon.

"Hell, it's the country, isn't it? What's wrong with getting back to nature when I'm on vacation?" she muttered, pulling off her hat.

"That's the spirit," he coaxed.

"But I'm keeping my T-shirt on," she told him.

He seemed only too compliant. "Sure. Go right ahead."

She looked down at herself.

The sheer white T-shirt would be worse—or better, depending on the perspective—than being naked. Still, her sense of modesty wouldn't allow her to fling it off.

"You know, I think you're setting me up," she added warily.

"For what?" he whispered in her ear before he took her hand and pulled her on top of him into the swimming hole.

"You j-j-jerk!" she stammered, gasping at the frigid chill of Rocky Mountain melt water.

"Best to keep moving" was all he offered.

Enraged, she tried to dunk his head.

Laughing, he even let her a few times, as if it would be good for her to get her anger out.

"Bet you can't do this." He swam over to the wheel and held on to it for a few feet. Then he dove into the pool as if from a diving board.

"Oh, yeah?" she taunted, answering the challenge. She was shivering and acting like a child, but she had to admit, she couldn't remember ever feeling so free.

She held on to the churning wheel. After a couple of seconds, she pushed herself off and plunged into the dark, frigid pool.

When she came up for air, she screeched with laughter. "My God, it's c-c-cold!"

He went to her. Unbidden, his arms encircled her waist. His torso was like a branding iron against her, but she couldn't deny herself the welcome warmth.

"Is this how you've gotten all your girls? Through hypothermia?" she jabbed.

"Nope," he answered, looking down at her while they treaded water. "Whiskey always worked just fine. But I figured you'd be a tough pony to tame."

"Ha!" She pushed his head into the water and swam away.

To prove her point, she held on to the wheel, this time longer, then cannonballed him.

"You know," she said blithely, swimming on her back, "this is fun. I'm actually getting used to the temperature of the water."

"Unfortunately, once you get out, you freeze all over again." His gaze followed her.

"Can't wait." She splashed him, he nearly splashed back.

She laughed and was almost grateful when he took her waist again and warmed her.

"I have a confession," she sputtered, wiping the water from her eyes. "You wouldn't know it from what I do for a living, but I was a tomboy as a child. I always wanted an older brother, too. To do stuff like this. Now I kinda feel like I have one."

He pressed her closer. "I hate to tell you this, but I have no intention of being your older brother."

She looked at him. The moonlight sparkled across the water and upon the droplets that clung to his chest hair. He seemed sexier by the minute, and yet, no warning bells went off in her head.

She feared it might still be the whiskey.

"No, really," she insisted. "That was a compliment. I always wanted some guy friends to pal around with. I thought after five years of marriage that I'd get some companionship from my husband, but, boy, was I wrong!'' She smiled and gave him a little splash. ''This has been just what the doctor ordered.''

''Good,'' he answered in a husky tone, just staring at her.

''What?'' she asked, her words lazy and maybe even more inviting than she had intended.

''How'd you meet him?''

''Who?'' she asked, suddenly blank.

''Your husband.''

She almost laughed. ''At a book reading. Can you imagine anything more dull? That should have been the first warning, huh?'' She treaded water. ''Then, after that, he decided to write the Great American Novel, and like the infatuated fool, I did everything I could to support him. Even when he took all the money I had to give with my little business, I still believed he deserved more. I always thought he needed to travel more, to prop up his surroundings so he could write. I had to be the perfect helpmate, and that meant to give and give and give 'till I and everything else was spent. But I wasn't going to end up alone and poor like my mom.'' She released a wry smile. ''So since I'm alone now, I work 24/7, so I won't be poor, too.''

A long pause reigned when the only sounds were the creak of the wheel and the soft splash of falling water.

To relieve the tension, she flicked some water at

him. "So how d'ya like that for a sisterly confession?"

"Nothing sisterly about it."

"No?" she asked, raising her damp eyebrows. "You think I'd confess that to a date? I don't think so. That's for brothers only, pal."

His stare only grew more intense. Even in the dimness of the moonlight, she could see his gaze tracing every shadow of emotion that swept past.

"Can't be my little sister," he instructed, his voice low, like a seductive growl. "Impossible. Because, first of all, I already have one. Her name's Becky."

"I'm sure she's lucky—" she stammered, losing her train of thought beneath that dark stare.

"And second, I never wanted to do this to her."

His arms tightened. He crushed her against his chest. Slowly his hard lips descended upon hers. The heat of his mouth shocked her. The delicious contrast of her cold lips and his warm tongue made her release an involuntary moan.

His kiss deepened and she could taste the whiskey on his breath and smell the male scent of him. Against her will, she found her mouth opening to him, as if she was thirsty for him and all she wanted to do was drink. His broad warm chest coaxed like a blanket in the snow. It was all too much to resist, and she felt herself folding into it as if she could crawl inside the fortress of it and be safe and warm forever—

His tongue ran down the slick wet skin of her neck giving her chills that had nothing to do with the Montana night air. Instinctively she crushed her breasts against his chest, her nipples, puckered with cold, brushed erotically against the wet fabric of her bra and the hard warmth of his pectorals.

Her hand slid down his back and pressed his buttock. Groaning, he slid her fingers to his groin, enticing her to feel his arousal. But she knew he was hard and ready without having to verify it. He pressed himself against her, his maleness like a police baton.

She pulled back, suddenly knowing she was in over her head.

The weariness in her eyes seemed to stop him too. His warmth was suddenly gone. She seemed to awaken from a dream, and found herself in the arms of a snowman. He pulled away from her, the eyes still staring, but this time with accusation and censure.

"We've got to go," he said abruptly, pulling her out of the water as if she were nothing but a rag doll.

"Why?" she gasped, disoriented by his moods and the lash of stinging cold air on her wet body.

"Do what's good for you, girl. Get your clothes on," he answered gruffly.

She looked at him. Every tight line of his buttocks was visible in the sheer wet cotton of his boxers.

He turned around to scowl at her. She held her breath. If what she saw between his legs was the result of cold shrinkage, she doubted she could handle it, even then.

"You want some now?" he demanded.

She gasped and shook her head.

"Then, get your clothes on." He turned to scoop up his jeans and shirt.

She fumbled for her jeans. Sodden and shivering, she could hardly pull them on.

"You can put your boots on in the truck." He led her by the elbow to the pickup and helped her into the cab.

Seated next to her, he flipped the switch for the diesel and started the engine.

"W-w-was it something I did?" she stammered.

He glanced at her, his face a stone mask in the dashboard light.

"I thought we were having fun—"

He stopped her. "Know what a grizzly feels like when it wakes up?"

She shook her head, her eyes wide.

"He's hungry," he growled. "So hungry he can't think of anything but what it is that he wants."

"And what do you want?" Her words came out in a frightened whisper.

He took one hard look at her. He didn't have to speak.

Even she heard the word in the silence, the long, echoing word, damning her and praising her in a monosyllabic curse.

You.

Three

"**A** dead varmint. Yep. That's what she looks like." Hazel's words penetrated the fog in Lyndie's mind.

"It's awake! It's awake! Hallelujah!" Ebby, Hazel's longtime cook, a tall raw-boned woman who'd ranched a hundred head of cattle and five sons all on a widow's pension, stood over the bed.

Hazel peered over Ebby's silver tray of coffee and toast. "Yep. There's life in her still. I see her glaring at me."

Lyndie sat up in bed. Her head pounded. She winced.

"Have a good stomp at the mill, did we?" Ebby tsked while she set down the breakfast tray.

"I'll never drink whiskey again," Lyndie moaned.

"Is it the whiskey you regret, or the man?" Hazel asked.

"Oh, please say it's the whiskey." Ebby clucked. "Even old hens like us dream about men like Bruce Everett."

Lyndie eyed both women woefully. "I was set up. And which one of you did it? Was it—Hazel?" she accused.

Hazel smiled like a Cheshire cat. "Live life to bursting, I always say. But I didn't think you'd go and do it the first minute you were off the yoke, dear. Still, you're a McCallum through and through. You'll find your way. We McCallums always do."

"Hazel, promise me for the rest of this trip that you'll refrain from mentioning the words *whiskey* and *men.*"

Lyndie wobbled to her feet, clad in pink satin pajamas of her own label. The memory of the night before was coming to her in waves like the water from a gristmill. She recalled the awkward silence in the pickup as Bruce drove her to the Lazy M. It was almost as if Mitch and Katherine had been in the truck cab with them, casting their pall. After a chilly farewell, she'd crawled to her bed, vowing to forget about Bruce Everett forever.

And then the nightmares came.

She'd had them all night long.

She'd be at the grocery store, the accountant's, in line for a movie—then she'd look down and see herself as if in a mirror. Her white T-shirt was wet and transparent, outlining each half-dollar mauve nipple, and her sodden hair was plastered against her forehead like a water nymph.

But what was worse than the rush of self-consciousness and the gasps of the onlookers was the emotional crash that followed.

She'd cover herself, but everywhere she ran to hide, she found Bruce Everett and his chilled gaze drilling into her, and the word that forced her back into feeling, thinking, yearning womanhood.

You.

She clamped her eyes closed and tried to erase it from her mind. Opening them again, she glanced at Ebby and Hazel and announced, "I'd better check work. I've got a lot to do before noon, when we've got to go to that—that—" she shuddered at the thought of seeing Bruce Everett again "—that dude ranch."

"Noon?" Ebby exclaimed, giving Hazel a raise of her eyebrows. "It's two hours past that and then some. We thought maybe you never slept in New Orleans—vampires and all that kind of stuff."

"What?" Lyndie grabbed the silver alarm clock next to the bed. She nearly screamed in horror at the time. "I had an investors' meeting online at eleven.'' She put her aching head in her hands. ''Now I've messed everything up.''

''Dear, cheer up. You're on vacation. Forget about that shop for now. You've got the dude ranch to go to,'' Hazel comforted.

''But I might have lost a whole pool of potential investors. There goes my expansion plans. There goes everything.'' Lyndie wanted to cry.

''The only expansion plan you should be thinking about is your horizon. Go out there, dear, and have fun at the ranch.''

Lyndie moaned anew. ''Even that's gone to hell. According to the Mystery Dude Ranch schedule, we were supposed to have our first trail ride at two. Now I've missed it and I'll be...'' She cringed. ''...*noticed.*''

Ebby shrugged. ''Young people nowadays. You're all just a bunch of flapdoodles.''

Hazel held out her hand to Lyndie. ''C'mon, gal. You're a McCallum. And McCallums never know defeat.''

Lyndie got out of bed, but she had the sinking feeling she'd regret it. It was the kind of day that she expected even her horoscope to read: Do not venture beyond the covers for destruction awaits you.

And certainly, after her experience with her father's cheating, and then with Mitch, there was no greater destruction facing her than a cool-eyed man with hunger in his stare. Hunger that seemed only for her.

Hazel drove Lyndie to Mystery Dude Ranch and left her at the bunkhouse, aching head and all. The ranch was deserted. It seemed everyone was on the trail. With nothing else to do, Lyndie checked her e-mail.

She'd received several urgent messages from her accountant. The last was the notice that the investors she had painstakingly courted for months had all declined to be involved. There was no money coming in for the expansion because she hadn't been able to convince anyone she was serious enough.

Nothing was further from the truth.

She ate, drank and breathed All for Milady. The shop was everything to her. Her entire life. Especially since she and Mitch split up.

And now, because of one foolhardy night, she was bound to fail.

Depressed, she turned off her laptop.

She looked at the pine log bed and wanted to throw herself upon it in a fit of tears. But it was no use. She'd cried a flood of tears over Mitch, and they were not the answer. The only thing that was, was diligent hard work.

Clearly, as exhausted as she was, she was still not working hard enough. The only thing left for her was to pack her bags, return to New Orleans and rededicate herself to her business. It was the only way to find happiness. It was the only thing she could control, and she was doing a poor job of even that.

Her head still feeling as if it was being breached by a ballpeen hammer, she retrieved her suitcase from under the bed and unzipped it.

"You're late."

She looked up to see Bruce Everett standing in her doorway, a scowl on his handsome face.

He looked wonderful, of course. Dust from the trail clung to his well-worn chaps. His face was hard and unshaven, but it only added to the overall ruggedness of his appearance. His gray stare pinned her down with icicles.

"I know. I'm sorry," she offered, unable to hate him when she was so busy hating herself right now. "But I've realized I've got to get back to New Orleans today. Business."

She tried to ignore him and the uncomfortable way he made her feel, by grabbing her clothes from the bureau and stuffing them in the suitcase.

"No planes today. You won't be going. So let's get on the trail. That way you can keep up with the others." His words brooked no discussion.

She looked up from her packing. "What do you mean there's no plane today? If I can get to Salt Lake City or Denver—"

"There's no plane out from the airport today. It's

Sunday and this is Mystery—a small airport. And if you're thinking Hazel can drive you to the next nearest airport, she can't. It'd take too long, and then you'd miss that flight. So you're stuck here for at least a day. Let's go.''

She stood, dumbfounded. He motioned the way out of the bunkhouse. Numbly, she followed, feeling like a canary in a cage.

''We'll start in the corral today. No time for a trail ride.'' His gaze slid to her. ''I'll get you through all you need to know for tomorrow's ride.''

''But what's the point of a riding lesson if I'm leaving?'' She wondered how he was going to get around that fact.

He stopped and stared at her. ''Why do you have to leave?''

''I told you. Business,'' she answered coolly.

He lifted one dark eyebrow. ''You mean that silent partner stuff? You don't need it.'' He took her arm and led her to the corral.

She widened her eyes. ''Thank you, Mr. Know-It-All, but I really think since it's my store, and my concern, maybe I should be the one to determine that.''

She had such a visceral reaction to his expression, she actually took a step backward.

But it was no use. He took her by the arm and led her to a pretty palomino mare.

"Get on up there," he ordered. "Here, I'll give you a leg up."

Before she could utter another word, his arm went around her waist. She was reminded of their kiss at the gristmill and a strange electricity crackled through her. Their gazes met for a millisecond—too quick to even measure—but the current between them increased to unbearable wattage.

He drew his hand down her thigh until he gripped her shin, then he hoisted her on top of a solid palomino. Her leg still felt the heat of his touch even through the thick denim of her jeans.

"Name's Girlie. Fitting for you, I think," he mumbled, glancing at her with those cold eyes.

The male-to-female reaction was only heightened by his words. She didn't want to feel feminine or "girlie" with him around. She wanted to be neutral, invisible, sexless, particularly around this swaggering tall cowboy who seemed to sniff out a woman's vulnerability to the opposite sex like a bloodhound on the trail of an escapee.

Shaken and discombobulated, Lyndie petted the pretty animal's flowing yellow mane in an attempt to ignore him. The palomino tossed her head, rattling her rider.

Frightened, Lyndie lashed out at her keeper. "Hey, I really don't need a riding lesson when I'll be taking off tomorrow—"

He ignored her. "The Western horse has five gaits—a walk, a jog..." he rambled.

Lyndie hardly listened. Her head still pounded, and now she was seeing red.

The man was a lout.

First he tried to seduce her by taking her skinny-dipping, then he rejected her, now he was bossing her around as if she were the employee, not him.

The nerve.

"Got it?" he demanded when his speech was through.

"Got it," she spat, eyeing him balefully.

"Then, walk." He bit out his words like a Marine commander. His lips twisted in a taunt. "Just squeeze your thighs. Both horses and men respond to that command."

Her breath caught in her throat by the innuendo. Unable to deal with him anymore, she squeezed Girlie as hard as she could, choosing to focus on her rather than him. The mare went forward with a jolt. She nearly got tossed on her backside as the mare began to jog.

Lyndie tossed Bruce a baleful stare. Inside she was steaming.

He laughed. His white teeth flashed. "Just like a city slicker, wanting to lope before she can walk."

He went to the mare and tugged on her bridle to slow her down.

The animal went down to a manageable walk.
Lyndie caught her breath and renewed her nerve.

In the lull, she studied him as he stood watching
from the center of the ring.

*It's as if he's running from something—and I just
want to see him stop and turn around, is all.* Lyndie
recalled Hazel's words describing Bruce.

She looked down at the golden horse beneath her.
Instinctively, she trusted the mare. The animal was
responsive and gentle. Lyndie thought she could actually get used to being on her back, but that
wouldn't be a luxury she would allow right now.

Hazel may think Bruce needed to quit running,
but as she rode round and round the ring, his pierc-
ing icicle gaze heating her, she knew she was the
one who wanted to run.

And just like the domineering male he was, all he
would let her do right now was walk.

Okay, so she fell off a few times.

Big whoop, Lyndie thought as she limped back
to her bunkhouse. The whole experience racked up
to zero, anyway, since all she was going to do was
pack up her bags and leave.

However, she had to admit she did like Girlie.

The quarter horse had shown the patience of Job
during the lesson. While Lyndie had bounced and
shifted, desperate to gain her equilibrium, the palomino had been steadfast.

Even Lyndie knew the reasons she'd fallen off: her own thick head and her inability to take instruction from Mr. Bruce Everett.

Exhausted, she flung herself onto the pine bed and booted up her computer, oblivious to the dust on her jeans and boots. Going online, she checked her e-mail to see how her accountant was faring in her absence.

There was an urgent message from him, and she knew the man had to be panicking since there was no cash to pay off the new orders.

She was surprised to read his message:

Lyndie,
No worries! A new investor, the MDR Corporation, came forward with quadruple the cash we thought we'd need for the expansion. MDR heard about the deal and has assured us the money will be wired first thing Monday morning.

We can look over the deal and sign all the documents when you return at the end of the month.

In the meantime, I insist you have a great vacation because I am now proceeding with mine.

All is extremely well in the Big Easy!
Rick

Lyndie read the message twice. She had a thousand questions for Rick Johnstone, CPA, so she quickly picked up her cell phone.

"Rick, this is Lyndie," she said when he answered. "Tell me, tell me," she pleaded.

He laughed. "We got a faxed letter practically begging us to take MDR as a silent partner."

"But who are they?" she asked.

"We'll look the gift horse in the mouth when you get back." He chuckled. "I only know you must have converted someone out west, because the corporation's address is there in Mystery."

She stared at the phone as if she were hearing things.

"Lyndie?"

"Uh-huh." She frowned. She knew exactly who had bailed her out.

Great-aunt Hazel. The woman owned most of Mystery. She had plenty of ready cash on hand to become a silent partner in a business.

But Lyndie couldn't accept it. Hazel was family. She couldn't take the risk with the money if there was family involved. Her mother had been too proud for charity, and Lyndie was, too.

She rubbed her still-pounding head. "Let me think on it. I'll try and be back tomorrow."

"It's a good deal, Lyndie. But do what you have to do."

They hung up.

She sat on her bed for a long time.

She couldn't let Hazel be her guardian angel. The hole she was in, she had dug herself. The expansion had already been in the works when Lyndie found out she didn't have enough capital. Both she and Rick knew she would have to sell off Milady to pay her new debts if they couldn't raise new capital.

She would have to see Hazel tonight and refuse the money. Tomorrow she would fly out and begin the process again. Maybe this time it would work.

Now she just had to get a ride after dinner to Hazel's. And she would probably have to ask Bruce Everett to take her.

She moaned. Was there no saving face in front of the man?

Heaving a great sigh, she gathered her bath supplies.

Surely there was a cab company in Mystery. As soon as she soaked her sore muscles, she would find out how to call one. Then she could avoid asking anyone for favors, let alone being indebted to Bruce Everett and having to endure his damnable all-knowing gaze.

The plan sounded so good. On paper. Just like her investors.

"Heard a rumor Hazel's girl is leavin'." Justin Garth, the stable manager, said while the cowhands were gathered in the cookhouse.

Bruce looked up from his laptop. He kept track of his herd in eastern Montana by way of reports from his ranch.

"She's not going anywhere. She needs this vacation." He bit out the words, then went back to his computer screen.

"Not what I heard," Justin retorted, his handsome tanned face crinkled with suppressed laughter. "I heard she can't wait to beat a path out of Mystery since she went swimming with you at the mill. What happened, partner? Was it too cold to impress her, or what?"

All Justin got was a snarl. "I don't need to impress no woman from New Orleans. I'm sure she's seen more naked men at a tea party down there than most women see in a lifetime."

"So you both were naked, eh?" Justin whistled. Though short of stature, he was a bearish man with thick red hair and an easy grin, and he was usually considered the troublemaker in the lot.

"We weren't naked," Bruce said.

"Almost naked?"

Bruce finally laughed. He didn't confirm or deny the charge.

"She's sure a beauty, that one. I saw her at the stomp and near fell in love right then and there. And I'll bet she's headstrong, too, if Hazel's blood's in her."

Bruce frowned.

"Are you thinkin' a goin' for it? If not, I certainly wouldn't mind—" Justin stopped his offer dead.

Bruce's expression told him all he needed to know.

"Fine. Fine," the cowpoke finished. "But don't let me hear she's gone back to New Orleans without any Mystery hospitality. It would break my heart."

A snort was Bruce's response.

Justin looked at him working on the computer.

"It's about time you took a woman. I've never seen a grizzly so mean as you without one."

A shrug and then the words "I've quit hibernating" was the only answer Justin got.

If there was one thing Lyndie could say about Montana, it was that it certainly increased her appetite. Gone were the days of existing on a *café au lait* and a salad. The Mystery Dude Ranch's chuck wagon served steak, and she found she craved it like an anemic.

Filling her plate, she sat down at a rustic pine table in the middle of the lodge. There were maybe fifteen people at most making up the ranch's guests.

"Roger Fallon, and this is my wife, Annette." A bearded and bespectacled middle-aged man stood up at Lyndie's picnic table while she seated herself.

"I'm pleased to meet you," she replied, suddenly self-conscious of her heaping plate.

"We saw you at the stomp last night. We're from

London. Living the real cowboy life here, ain't we?'' Annette was a matronly, twinkle-eyed, bleached blonde with a contagious smile.

Lyndie liked them both immediately. There was something disarming about the couple. She thought perhaps it was the cowboy attire. Both had enthusiastically dressed for the trail, right down to the leather-fringed vests and red knotted kerchiefs.

''You've come far to ride a horse,'' Lyndie commented pleasantly.

''This is the best dude ranch in the U.S. How could we resist—despite the cost?''

Annette's words took Lyndie aback. She hadn't paid anything for the dude ranch; she figured Hazel had owned it, and just let her come. Now she wondered if she was even more indebted to the cattle baroness than she'd thought, for letting her take the place of a well-heeled, paying tourist.

''I— I have to confess I don't know much about the dude ranch,'' Lyndie said. ''My great-aunt, who lives here in Mystery, told me to come. She was convinced I was working myself to death, but that really wasn't so.''

Lyndie cut into the thick juicy filet still sizzling on her plate. She was mortified that Hazel might have allowed the Mystery Dude Ranch to take a loss on her. She'd assumed the ranch was Hazel's, to do with as the cattle baroness wished.

''The cowboys here are supposed to be the best

in the state. But Bruce Everett was recommended to us from Tokyo to Timbuktu," Roger Fallon commented with a charming smile. "We've waited five years on the list to get to come here. How about you?"

Color crept into Lyndie's cheeks.

She'd had no idea Mystery Dude Ranch was such a desirable destination. If anything, she figured Hazel had let her come because the ranch was desperate for customers.

"I really don't know anything about a list. As I said, my great-aunt got me up here." Lyndie chewed her steak, hoping they could change the subject.

"So you have real relations here who are cowboys?" Annette seemed amazed. "How utterly fascinating. You have no idea how far the average Londoner will go to live the life of a cowboy for just a week."

"I had no idea," Lyndie conceded.

"Oh, darling. Look who's here!" Annette jabbed her husband.

All at the table looked to the chuck wagon. Bruce Everett was at the grill, getting his steak.

"He is the most fantastical person, don't you agree?" Roger said to Lyndie. "All those rodeos. All those championship belt buckles. I feel like we're living a Clint Eastwood film with him around.

The ranch's fees were worth double what we paid, just to experience what he can show us.''

Lyndie glanced at Bruce.

He glanced back.

A strange unwanted shiver shook her very core. As much as she fought it, consciously, valiantly, she was succumbing. Desire crept up on her with every swagger of his hips, with every flash of his lazy smile. If she didn't fight it, she might fall altogether.

''What can he show us? I'm not that familiar with him.'' Lyndie turned her attention back to her steak.

''Why, he's considered one of the best cattle breeders in all of the West. He has a ranch a couple hundred miles from here. And he does have a legend around him,'' Annette chimed in.

''We read that he once saved a pair of grizzly cubs from the highway by scooping a cub up in each arm and running them to safety. The man's strong, because even a baby grizzly's bloody heavy.''

''And what did the mother think of all that?'' Lyndie couldn't help but ask.

''She was right smitten with him, like all the other of her sex,'' Roger finished. ''She just put her cubs in check and disappeared to the other side of the highway.''

''Certainly sounds like a tall tale to me,'' Lyndie commented drily.

''Miss Clay. May I have the pleasure?''

She looked over her shoulder and found the subject of their discussion standing—no, looming—over her.

"Mr. Everett," she acknowledged as he sat next to her with his steak and his thick, muscular thigh pressing against her own, reminding her of all the things she was lonely for.

Annette and Roger both gaped.

Lyndie could only offer a weak smile.

After all, there was so much to deny, and so very little to acknowledge.

"Have you fully recovered from last night?" Bruce asked.

Annette looked ready to swoon and Roger certainly needed to close his jaw.

"Have you met Roger and Annette?" Lyndie asked in a perky tone. "They're from London. Big fans."

Bruce nodded. "I met you on the trail. You both have a good sense of balance. That's to be appreciated in a greenhorn."

"Th-tha-thank you," Roger stuttered, his salt-and-pepper beard twitching with pleasure.

"We were just telling Miss Clay here how wonderful the ranch is," Annette added. "She doesn't seem to be as familiar with it as most."

Bruce slid Lyndie a glance. "She'll find her way. Besides, she's come highly recommended."

"By my great-aunt Hazel," Lyndie finished, trying to set it straight.

"Yes, Miss Clay is a businesswoman. She doesn't feel the need to get back in touch with her natural side."

Bruce dug into his steak as if it were his last meal. Lyndie watched that hard, punishing mouth tear into the meat, and the memory of his kiss made her melt from the pit of her stomach all the way down to her knees.

"Never lose touch, my dear," Annette said. "For there's nothing like a pink mountain sunset, or the sight of an elk with her young, to remind you what's truly important."

"And that is?" Lyndie prompted, clinging to any subject that would free her mind from the fiery press of the muscular male thigh against hers.

"God. The spirit. Connection. All that and more," her husband added.

Lyndie mulled over the words. They were poetic to her hungry soul, but the wounded part of her knew the words and their substance were out of reach.

Releasing a sad little smile she said, "Unfortunately, there are no spreadsheets and inventory in those mountains, and that's what's got a choke-hold on me. I'm afraid I'll be flying home tomorrow. I've had a business emergency."

"Oh, no!" Annette cooed.

Lyndie turned to Bruce. "Which reminds me. I'll need a cab to go to Hazel's tonight. What's the name of the taxi company around here?"

"I'll take you," he said.

She held up her hand. "No, no. I couldn't impose—"

"You're a guest at this ranch. There's no imposition."

She went back to her steak, suddenly devoid of appetite. Now she was going to have to be alone with the man again. But at least she'd made it clear she wanted no favors from him.

She pushed the steak away. "Well, then, if you'll excuse me, I'll get ready to see Hazel. It was nice meeting you," she said to the British couple.

"I hope things change so you can stay," Annette added.

Lyndie smiled and shrugged her shoulders helplessly. "I guess playing is for others—and not the self-employed—"

"Could have surprised me last night," Bruce interjected, nonchalantly taking a bite of his steak.

Roger and Annette exchanged a delighted look.

"Well, I— I guess I'm not quite as used to whiskey as the locals," Lyndie stammered, lamely trying to save her reputation.

"Then, you should drink more often," Bruce commented, clearly holding back a grin.

Lyndie wanted to punch him.

Instead, she turned to leave, an old saying following her out the door. *If a girl is brave enough, she can do without a reputation.*

All she knew was that a girl sure had to be brave around Bruce Everett.

Four

Lyndie said nothing during the ride to Hazel's. She sat silent, once more watching Bruce's Adonis profile by the green dashboard light.

The truck pulled through the wrought-iron gates of the Lazy M ranch. Perfunctorily, Bruce held the truck door for her and walked her to the entrance.

"C'mon in!" Hazel announced when she answered the door. "Well, don't you two look like a fine surprise. Giddy-ap in here and let me look at you both!"

Lyndie opened her mouth to protest that only she needed to speak with Hazel, but suddenly she realized how rude that would appear. After all, Bruce had driven her to the Lazy M, and he was one of Hazel's friends.

She closed her mouth, and along with Bruce stepped inside Hazel's antique-filled parlor.

Portraits and tintypes of McCallums, her very own ancestors, stared back at her from the walls. It seemed even they were holding their collective breath.

"Ebby, get us some refreshment, won't you? We got company," Hazel said when Ebby appeared at the elaborately carved walnut pocket doors.

Ebby looked more than pleased to see them. "Right away! Coming right away!" she promised, wringing her hands excitedly on her white apron.

"What brings you two out here to see me?" Hazel asked, gesturing to the silk-covered parlor love seat.

Once again, Lyndie felt set up, but somehow it was a trap of her own making. She sat next to Bruce on the love seat.

The tiny Victorian piece was not made for modern figures. She found she was practically sitting on Bruce's lap once he splayed his legs and accepted the brandy from Ebby.

Deciding to be out with it, Lyndie declined refreshment and said, "Hazel, I can't let you do it. I found out about the MDR Corporation and your generous investment in Milady, but I can't accept it. It's risky—and even as hard as I know I'll work for it, I can't accept that there's even the possibility of losing your money. So I'm declining—''

''You're declining the offer of good honest cash?'' Bruce interrupted. ''What kind of business-woman are you?''

Lyndie's temper snapped. ''Look, Mr. Everett, in all respect, I don't need your opinions. This really is between Hazel and me.''

Hazel glanced from one to the other. She seemed to want to say something, but the words eluded her—a rarity where Hazel McCallum was concerned.

''Lyndie, dear, I don't cotton to unwanted opinions any more than you do, but I think Bruce is right,'' she began hesitantly. ''It's good honest cash. It's what you need to expand. And it's also what you need in order to take this vacation and get a break from the work that—according to your mother—is grinding you into the ground.''

''I'll be fine,'' Lyndie declared. ''But I couldn't live with myself if the business took a downturn and I couldn't give you a profit, let alone repay the debt.''

''You won't lose it. It's not a possibility,'' the cattle baroness said firmly.

''But what if—''

Hazel cut her off.

''Lyndie, let this settle it. Take the MDR Corporation's cash for now. When you've had a rest up here and your time at the dude ranch is up, you can go back to New Orleans and find new investors.''

"But that may take time. I should go now—"

Hazel put up her hand. "I won't hear of it." Her notorious Prussian-blue eyes glittered with mischief. "Humor an old woman, will you, Lyndie."

Lyndie wanted to roll her eyes. Hazel had caught her in a web but good.

"It's only for a few weeks. You'll be home before the month is up, and the same problems will be there waiting for you when you do."

Setting her jaw, Lyndie agreed. "Fine. But I'm paying interest on the money, five percent over prime. That's more than the bank pays."

Hazel laughed. Even Bruce looked as if he was biting back a chuckle.

"Excellent. Then, we have an agreement? You'll take MDR's cash and stay here as long as you promised?" Hazel's silver eyebrows went up.

"Yes."

Lyndie released her breath. She didn't know how she was going to pay the interest, let alone procure new financing, but she would do it if taking the money for a time would make her great-aunt happy.

"Now do have a cookie. It's my mother's recipe. Made with essence of violet—quite the rage in eighteen ninety-five." Hazel held out a hand-painted plate filled with pale butter cookies.

Even though she had no appetite, Lyndie took one.

For the next twenty minutes, Hazel made small talk. Finally, when the parlor clock chimed, Bruce rose from the settee. In his flannel shirt and jeans, he looked like a giant in the beautiful parlor.

"Part of ranch life is getting up early, Hazel, so if you don't mind?" He reached for his ubiquitous black Stetson, which Lyndie hadn't noticed him place on a nearby table.

"Yes, that's right." The gleam in Hazel's eyes danced. "And this girl of mine needs rest and lots of it. Now, you promise to get her to bed right away."

Lyndie was so exhausted that she'd kissed Hazel good-night and gone out the front door before she realized exactly what the old girl had said. Or, in truth, what the old girl had *meant*.

"She's downright wicked, isn't she," Lyndie said in a quiet tone as they pulled out of the Lazy M ranch.

Bruce smiled. "She's one of a kind, that's for sure. I always wanted a woman like Hazel."

"She's available, you know," she answered archly.

He looked at her. His eyes warmed in the pale green light. "I know, but unfortunately for me, Hazel's out of the reckoning for having babies—and I want lots of them."

His comment shocked her. She didn't want to think of him as a family man. She'd wanted children herself, but Mitch had always put it off. After she'd discovered the true nature of his character, she was almost relieved they hadn't had children. But that had left her wanting. A family, a husband, children. It didn't seem like anything she was entitled to. Her mother hadn't gotten it; neither, it seemed, would she.

But then, here was this cowboy sitting next to her, telling her he had the same yearning. It made him way too appealing. It made him dangerous.

"What're you thinking? You don't like babies?" He returned to the road.

She shook her head. "Love them. Don't have any—hear they're a lot of trouble."

"That it?"

She almost laughed. She didn't know what else to say. Men just didn't talk like this in the city. An urban man was more apt to show a woman the keys to his sports car than look in her mouth to see if she was good breeding stock.

"What more is there?" she asked, quashing her trepidation on the subject.

"Well, how many kids would you want?"

She tried to hide her surprise. "It depends, doesn't it?"

"On what?"

"On the father." She looked at him as if he were crazy.

He nodded. "The father's good. Go on that one. Then, how many?"

"Look, I'm not the baby-factory type. I mean, I've certainly got good wide hips—I know it every time I go to buy a pair of pants—but my idea of child-rearing isn't just like having puppies. They're expensive, you know. Kids."

She hoped that might set him straight. After all, he had a good enough job at Hazel's dude ranch, but he certainly couldn't tack a wife and kids onto the back of the bunkhouse.

"I never thought of it that way," he said pensively. "My parents had seven kids. Somehow they managed. They saw to it there was food on the table and love in the house. That kinda taught me to believe that if something's important, you can't think about the cost."

She gave him an ironic smile. "I'm afraid I can't afford idealism. My mother raised me alone and it was difficult. So difficult that I'm determined not to repeat it. Besides, I have to confess I'm a little preoccupied with fiscal responsibility right now—as you know, since you were sitting through my whole conversation with Hazel."

"You worry too much about that business."

Her sigh was involuntary. "The business is all I have. It's what holds me together. I work hard. Hell, for the last couple of years I've done nothing but work hard.''

"But you have to play, too.''

There was no arguing with his logic.

"You don't have time to play when you're drowning,'' she said grimly.

He looked over at her.

"Then, let someone save you.''

She let out a bitter laugh. "No one saved my mother from being a single mom, and if I'd had a child with Mitch I'd be in the same lonely sinking boat. So, no thanks.''

"In my world, we don't abandon family.''

She let the words fall into silence. The temptation was so great to believe him, to let someone else be strong. But the fear it aroused was worse than the comfort.

Something was on his mind, she could see it. She would have to put him off now, or it would be hard going for her, she just knew it.

Stammering, she confessed, "I guess what happened to my mom and what happened with Mitch— well, it's just too hard to believe in commitment and love and devotion— It's hard to allow yourself the luxury of believing, when you've had to watch them being taken away.''

He stared at her between glances at the road. "Look, last night at the mill… It was…'' His words trailed off.

"Oh, I know. What in the world was I doing? I guess I'm a little crazy right now," she dismissed, embarrassed.

"Hazel wants you to let loose. Forget about that shop for a while. It'd do you good."

She rubbed her forehead. A headache was definitely coming on. "I appreciate the advice, but really, what's it to you?"

"At the mill—with you—I realized I need to play, too." His confession was harsh and bitter. She couldn't help but be moved by it. His devotion to Katherine proved he was probably more steadfast than Mitch had been, and it suddenly made her ashamed of her conclusions about him. He was hurting, too.

Gently, she began, "Hazel told me what happened to your girlfriend. I'm sorry. It must have been terrible."

He said nothing.

The silence became oppressive.

"Look," she began with a deep breath, "you can't go by my opinions. I'm the creature of my own experience. But you—well, you sound like you had a great family life. So I hope you do start playing. You deserve it, after what you've been through. You've got a lot to give."

"And you give too much. You need to learn to take," he urged.

She closed her eyes and shook her head. "Sounds so good, but I'm way too much of a coward. Sorry."

She was relieved that they'd turned into the dude ranch.

"Well, thank you for the ride. Let me know if I owe you anything—for gasoline or whatever." She couldn't think of anything else to say.

The truck pulled up to her bunkhouse. He put it in Park and turned to her. "What was he like? Your husband?"

The question took her aback. "He was—he was, well, I guess he was great at the beginning. I certainly thought I loved him. But then he turned into a jerk." She laughed darkly. "Yep, that's about the long and short of it."

He took her chin in his strong hand and their gazes locked. "He took the play out of you. He stole it just like a thief steals a diamond bracelet. You've got to get it back. It was yours and you need it."

Her stomach knotted. His touch left a feather-like arousal in her loins. His words left her on the verge of tears.

Steeling herself, she said, "Yes, he stole from me. But how can I get it back? I can't afford another diamond bracelet."

"Let someone else give you one."

She finally had a way out of the emotional maze he was putting her through. "Again, that sounds perfect. Just like the old line about how to be a millionaire—you know, you find a job that pays a million an hour, work for an hour, and there you go.'' She laughed.

"But I have news for you, Mr. Everett, it just doesn't work that way. I could get a million guys to promise me the world, but what will I really get other than an overactive libido?''

"Sometimes men keep their promises," he retorted.

"Maybe. But rule me out of that game. I've got too much work to do. At least my shop might take care of me in my old age. You, from what Hazel says about your youth, might be the type I couldn't count on until dawn.''

His jaw tightened. "I can go past dawn. You wanna test me?''

Her breath caught.

He let go of her chin.

"Good night, Miss Clay. We're hitting the trail early, so I heartily recommend you get some rest.''

She looked at him for a moment, then let herself out of the truck.

He took off in a cloud of dust.

Confused, she let herself into her bunkhouse room.

As she stripped and pulled back the covers, she wondered why she was even bothering. She knew she wasn't going to get any sleep that night. And even if she did doze off, the only thing she was going to dream of was Bruce Everett.

And wolfish white smiles that promised pleasure and damnation with one lopsided grin.

Droopy-eyed, Lyndie reined Girlie left, to follow the rest of the pack. They'd been at the trail for over an hour when they'd come to a crossroads.

"Not there. Don't ever go there," Justin instructed the group as they were about to take the wrong trail.

"What's up there?" Lyndie asked, tagging to the rear with Justin.

The trail-man only looked distant. "Som'un bad happened on that trail. We don't use it anymore."

Lyndie strained to see up the winding trail as far as she could. Mini avalanches of rock littered the path. The trail seemed to become almost vertical as it wound up the mountain into the snow.

A shiver went through her. Somehow she knew that was the path on which Katherine had lost her life.

She stared ahead at Bruce.

He seemed pointedly oblivious of the forbidden path. Instead, like any good guide, his attention was on his riders and the condition of the trail ahead. But he sat his horse with a stiffer back than usual, and Lyndie wondered if passing the fork in the trail hit a raw spot within him.

"Does anyone ever go up there anymore?" she asked Justin.

He only shook his head. "When the boss is in a temper he goes, but only then."

Lyndie returned her attention to the trail, her thoughts far away.

Roger and Annette were ahead of her on a couple of Appaloosas. Another two women, sisters, had signed up for the dude ranch from Los Angeles. They were outrageously flirtatious with their guide Justin, a burly redheaded cowboy who headed the trail, and Lyndie almost envied them.

They were playing.

Bruce abruptly went to the rear on his dun quarter horse, Beastie Boy. Girlie kept wanting to turn around and nip Beastie Boy. At one point, Lyndie laughed out loud: the horses seemed to be mirroring the tensions of their riders.

But she got nothing but a frosty stare from Bruce.

Finally they stopped at a stream where the chuck wagon met them for breakfast.

Justin held her horse while she dismounted. She had liked Justin on sight. The young man was every woman's idea of the boy next door. His grin was contagious, and she could see he had a soft spot for the ladies. Kim and Susan, the women from L.A., positively purred whenever he got within phero-mone distance.

"How you like it so far?" Justin asked Lyndie

while they were served bacon and eggs from the chuck wagon fire.

"Unfortunately, I missed yesterday's lesson, but I guess I can keep up," Lyndie offered.

"I'll be happy to give you time in the ring if you need extra schoolin'." Justin winked.

She couldn't hide her grin. There was something so wholesome about Justin. She could understand Kim and Susan's enchantment. He was what he was—outrageously on the prowl—as opposed to his boss, Bruce Everett, who was anything but comprehensible.

"I think I can muddle through, but thank you for the offer. I'll keep it in mind." Lyndie smiled and walked past Bruce.

He only scowled.

When she sat down against a tree trunk, she was dismayed when Bruce settled next to her.

"Sleep well?" he asked diabolically, as if he could read her dreams.

She tilted her mouth in a dismissive smile. "Why wouldn't I?" she challenged.

He cocked an eyebrow.

She dug into her eggs with a vengeance.

"Tonight's the rodeo. You up to it?" he mentioned, chewing on his bacon.

"Is that part of the program?" She buttered a biscuit.

"Absolutely."

"Then, I guess I can spare eight seconds."

He laughed, but then quickly sobered. Those gray eyes honed in on hers. "It's a long eight seconds. You ever ridden a bull?"

"No," she said truthfully.

"Then, you should try it." He went back to his breakfast.

The featherlight tingle traveled down her spine to her belly, and then lower.

She stared at him, at his long lean body, and the way his flannel shirt clung to each and every muscle bulge in his arm. She remembered the hair sprinkled across his chest and the trail of dark hair that promised to lead to pleasure.

The idea of staying on him for eight seconds thrilled and strangely terrified her.

The image didn't leave her mind the entire trip.

Even when she left Girlie in the paddock that evening, and she limped, saddle sore, back to her bunkhouse, she couldn't get the picture of eight seconds with Bruce Everett out of her head.

Five

"But he's so ridiculously male, Hazel. I can't take him seriously." Lyndie sat next to Hazel at the Mystery bull-riding rodeo, whispering.

"But that's what you don't understand, love. You're a McCallum. You don't have to take him seriously. You just have to relax and have some fun." Hazel stood and whooped for the latest eight-second winner.

"I admit he has a certain masculine charm..." Lyndie murmured.

"If he hired out the stud in him, he'd be richer than me," Hazel pronounced in her no-nonsense style.

Lyndie couldn't help but smile.

But the smile vanished the minute she caught Bruce's eye. He was at the gates, helping the bull riders onto their animals.

Being a champion bull rider himself, she figured, he probably had a lot of advice to give.

But to her, and her broken heart, he had nothing to offer. They were like night and day. He was racked with guilt over his ill-fated love; she was tormented by rage over her ex's betrayal. They didn't even have that in common.

"I admit he's rather attractive in a primordial caveman sort of way. But, Hazel, it would be wrong to use the man just for casual sex." Lyndie hoped the subject was finished.

"There are more happy marriages that began with nothing more than a bit of tomcatting around than I care to count." Once again Hazel was her usual blunt self.

"So what are you saying? Are you challenging me to get him into bed? You naughty woman."

Hazel put on her most serious face. "Of course, I'm not making such a lewd challenge." Hazel narrowed her eyes and studied her. Taunting her, the cattle baroness said, "I certainly understand if you can't attract him, my dear. You're the competitive type. Look at the business you're in. Retail. What could be more brutal? I couldn't ask you on your vacation to do something that's beyond your reach. It would be grossly cruel of me.''

Lyndie paused and stared at her great-aunt in amazement. ''You, Great-aunt Hazel, are an evil woman.''

Hazel smiled. ''You don't get to be my age, my dear, without understanding a thing or two about humanity.''

''I could get him into bed anytime I wanted to.''

''Prove it.''

Lyndie stared at her, confounded. ''Is the whole world conspiring against me?''

''You could do worse.''

''He's a cowboy with a chip on his shoulder the size of Wyoming.''

''Are you saying you won't accept the challenge?''

''The man is randy. If I offer sex, he'll take it.''

''They say he hasn't had a woman since Katherine. No one can fire him up. I don't expect you'll be able to, either.''

''It's not my job to play sex therapist, Hazel. He can hire that out.''

''Take a shot at him. If you fail, you fail.''

''What if I succeed, and he disappoints. What then? Are you going to reimburse me for the experience?''

Hazel turned to her, her expression gleeful. ''I'll

tell you what, my dear. If he disappoints, you don't have to repay MDR Corporation. Is that a deal?''

"Does my mother know what a wicked conspirator you are, Hazel?"

Hazel winked. "She never took my advice and look what happened—I always wanted her to marry that cowboy down in the valley."

Lyndie was speechless.

"You know what?" Lyndie said, pumped up on adrenaline and cheap beer as she stood next to Bruce at the gates.

Bruce paddocked the last prize-winning bull and wiped the dust from his eyes. "What?"

"I've been challenged by Hazel to seduce you. She doesn't think I can do it, but you know, I think I can. And if I succeed, she says she'll forgive my MDR Corporation debt."

He stared at her in the darkness of the paddock. She couldn't read his expression.

"Of course," she rambled, "I won't let her forgive the debt. I am a McCallum, after all, and I pay my debts back, but it would delight me to no end to prove her and her wicked matchmaking ways wrong. Would you go along with the gag?"

He stepped toward her. She leaned back against the metal tube fencing of the paddock until she nearly melted into it.

Still he came, pressing toward her, tall and intimidating, masculine and domineering.

"I'll go along with it. How far are we going?" He smiled.

"Well—not far enough for me to be a notch on your bedpost," she confirmed nervously.

"I'd rather you be tethered to my bedpost." He pressed his long lean body against hers.

His hard chest rammed against her soft, fulsome one. The contrast was almost more than she could bear. His steely arm clamped around her waist. She was captured.

She looked up at him, wondering how feminine wiles could ever tame such a male animal. Against her will, her breath quickened, and the fluttering in her belly became a heated dampness between her legs. She was no match for him when his very nearness caused her to tremble and melt.

"I just want out of a debt." She desperately tried to remain practical and detached.

"You know, there's a name for women like you. Money isn't always the key, is it?" His strong callused hand swept a wisp of hair from her eyes. His touch was fire.

She felt her cheeks heat with a blush. "Well, at least my price is more than you can pay."

He tilted back his head and laughed. "Don't be so sure of yourself. You'd be surprised what I can pay."

She smiled, valiantly trying to remain chummy even though his very scent was driving her to distraction; its earthiness, its darkness promised way more than she could handle.

Sobering, she said, "Look, this is our little joke. Play along with me, will you? For Hazel's sake?" she begged. "The woman's got her finger in every pot in this town. She really does need to fail once in a while so she will stay out of other people's business—including mine."

He put his face to hers. The heat of his breath warmed her cheek. "I'll play anything with you, girl, but what do I get if I win?"

She held his gaze. "You won't win."

"No?" he asked, his voice husky with desire.

"No," she affirmed, just before his lips came down on hers.

His mouth was hot and demanding, and the loneliness inside her took it like a rainstorm on scorched earth. His tongue pushed inside her hungry mouth and took away all thoughts of protest. He kissed her, and each second with him like this seemed to promise an eternity.

She knew she should push him away. A second wasn't an eternity, the rational side of her announced, but in his strong arms, she became nothing but gelatinous, quivering feeling. Her body turned so liquid, his embrace was the only thing holding her up.

And still she took his kiss, wondering who was the seducer and who the seducee. Everything got turned around where he was concerned.

His tongue licked a flame within her that melted even her most frigid parts.

Then the yearning came. Like a wind that passed through her very being, she wanted him, body and soul.

If they had not been in the shadows of a public arena she might have succumbed, right then and there.

"Is the battle mine?" he whispered harshly when he broke away.

"You won't win the war," she almost panted.

"Take it one fight at a time, love. You might find we're on the same side."

She wanted to laugh and cry at the same time. He inspired feelings inside her that she thought Mitch had destroyed. It was a shock to find she was still human and breathing and feeling, after all she'd been through.

It was also a shock to see she still held hope inside her, as if it were some kind of precious gem that, no matter how she denied its existence, still shone within her, everlasting.

"Maybe this wasn't such a good idea," she whispered, her hand across her mouth as if her lips still burned from the kiss. She wondered if she hadn't just yanked the tail of a sleeping beast.

"No, it's a great idea." He grinned, his mouth twisting in a lopsided way that made him—all steely muscles and steely eyes—look boyish.

Her gaze locked with his, and her confidence that she could control him faded with every excited beat of her heart.

"Do we start tonight?" He placed his hand on her waist and tried to kiss her again.

She nearly jumped. "Hey—let's not get carried away. I can't win right away. This has to look realistic."

"You mean you want a challenge?"

"Yes. This has to be a bit of a challenge, don't you think? Or Hazel won't believe it."

"I'll make Hazel believe it."

"That's the spirit," she said, her heartbeat calming.

"But I got no tolerance for teasing."

"What do you think I plan to do? Show up on the trail ride in just my panties and bra?" She laughed. "We're on a dude ranch. It'll be a miracle if you can still tell I'm a woman underneath all the dust and sweat in this place."

"You're the Panty Princess. Don't know what you sell in that shop down in New Orleans, but I know I don't want to be teased by it."

"This is just to fool Hazel," she countered. "I'm not really going to try and seduce you. You do understand that, don't you?"

He nodded.

Then, with a harsh whisper, he said, "I know. 'Cause I'm going to seduce you."

The crisp mountain air was something Lyndie was unused to. Riding Girlie along McCallum land, she revelled in the expansive view of rock and snow and velvety green valleys. They had breakfast on one side of the Continental Divide and lunch on the other. It was the first time in her life she'd tasted water that led to two different oceans.

"Having fun?" Annette asked, pulling her horse next to Lyndie's.

Lyndie smiled. "Having a blast. How about you?"

"It's a dream come true. I had no idea heaven was in Mystery, Montana."

Lyndie looked around her. It *was* heaven.

The last of the sun bronzed the face of the Divide, turning the snowtops to molten gold. Long blue shadows fingered up through the valleys to meet the thunderous cloudbank overhead. The scenery around her enticed and threatened like none other.

Except the cowboy who headed the trail.

Lyndie kept an eye on Bruce. He slouched deep in his saddle, clearly a veteran of trail rides. Beastie Boy kept a sure foot on the narrow trail.

It had been like this for three days. After her challenge, instead of playing along, all he did was ignore her. She was ready to give up the joke because it wasn't being played out too effectively. It was hard to pretend-seduce someone who didn't even look at you.

"Are you finally ready to embrace cowboy life, Lyndie?" Roger called out from behind.

"I'd have to be blind not to love it here," she called back, realizing it was true. For three days she'd done nothing but eat, sleep and drink horses. But through all the hard work, she found a peace that she had never known in New Orleans, crammed in her office at the back of the shop.

Perhaps there was something to the idea of getting back to nature. Montana touched the spirit inside of her, healing the wounds of urban life—the fast pace, the stress and the pollution.

Indeed, perhaps she was ready to embrace the cowboy life.

But she wouldn't be embracing the cowboy, she thought wryly as she watched the two sisters from L.A. flirt outrageously with their cowboy guides. Kim had taken up with Justin from the minute the woman's gaze landed on the redhead. That left Susan with no male companionship other than Bruce's.

And Susan saw to it that Bruce was never lonely. Heading out on the trail, Susan always maneuvered her horse directly behind Beastie Boy.

Lyndie didn't even dare go near them, for Girlie and Susan's horse were notorious fighters. She'd

been told by both Justin and Bruce that she must
not let Girlie anywhere near Susan's horse, and vice
versa, or they would suffer the consequences of
bucking, biting mares.

Which certainly killed any desire to get near
Bruce.

Lyndie was resigned to losing the bet with Hazel,
anyway.

That night at the rodeo proved she was out of her
league when it came to Bruce's seduction tactics.
He was the tomcat, she reminded herself, while she
had learned nothing about relationships except how
to play the good and devoted wife. Seduction had
not been emphasized in her love experience.

Besides, as she told herself bitterly, she clearly
wasn't all that good at it: her seductions hadn't kept
Mitch in the marital bed.

"We'll be leaving the trail early today. Storms
coming," Bruce announced, turning Beastie Boy as
if on a dime.

The rest of the riders followed, allowing Justin to
lead the way back.

"Damn lightning," Lyndie heard Bruce mutter
after the flash of light from the black sky.

Girlie's ears pricked forward. She began prancing.

A few seconds later, the delayed boom of thunder
sent the horse into a frenzy. The animal scrambled
along the path, but with the way ahead blocked by
Roger's horse, all she could do was dig her hooves

into the vertical side of the mountain, causing a rock slide.

"Whoa," Lyndie soothed, amazed she was still on the frightened animal.

"She's no good in a thunderstorm. Never has been. You'll have to come with me if you don't want to get hurt."

Lyndie heard Bruce before she felt his arm go around her. In one swoop, he'd taken her from the saddle and placed her on Beastie Boy. Then he grabbed Girlie's reins and calmed the skittish animal.

"That's her only flaw. Hates lightning," Bruce muttered.

"I have the same flaw. I hate it, too." Lyndie tried to relax against Bruce's torso, but the solid wall of muscle against her back unsettled her. Especially when he moved. Then every ripple seemed to burn into her back like a branding iron. And the rhythmic movement of the ride made her think of other kinds of activities she could do with him. His scent, too, was becoming all too addictive. Now mixed with the pungent scent of lodgepole pine and saddlesoap, he was a living aphrodisiac.

"Comfortable?" he asked, his mouth against her hair.

"I'm fine," she answered quickly—perhaps a bit too quickly.

He laughed, and her paranoia increased.

"We'll be back down the mountain soon. If you want another horse tomorrow, I'll get you one."

She looked back at Girlie. "I don't want another one. I like her."

"You might have to ride with me again."

Shrugging to free herself of unwanted sensations, she said, "I can handle her next time."

"I admit you're both pretty well matched. I ought to get Hazel to buy her for you."

"Buy her? And where would I keep her? In the French Quarter?" she quipped.

"You can keep her here."

His words made no sense at all. "Cowboy wisdom," she dismissed, rolling her eyes.

He laughed again, all the way down the mountain.

The rain came down in twisted sheets. The thunder and lightning show was magnificent against the black background of jagged mountains. Sitting on the porch rocker in front of her bunkhouse, Lyndie watched it all.

She had been unable to sleep, even though she was dog-tired. Her mind kept returning to Bruce, the way he had felt against her, the way he had looked at her at dinner.

Everyone ate in the lodge, family-style, on long ranch tables. He had yet to bless her with his company, but all through the meal, she swore he was staring at her from the other end of the table.

She wanted to know what he was thinking, which was probably her first error. Getting involved with anyone right now would be the worst thing for her, let alone getting entangled with a Montana dude ranch guide who hadn't had a woman in forever.

Sure, he could banter with her, match wits with her. And there was a certain animal attraction about him. He was all male. Sun and sweat and dust suited him.

But she had to quit thinking about him. There was no point in having an affair with a cowboy when she was going to ride into the New Orleans sunset.

Besides, getting involved again was the last thing she needed. Healing would come only when she could shrug off the pain of what Mitch did to her. Bruce Everett wasn't the medicine man to do that. She would need a real relationship; she would need love and commitment.

A brief physical affair would only leave her longing. And she had felt enough longing to last a lifetime.

Her mind entrenched in darkness, she almost didn't notice the crackle of the power lines. Suddenly the entire ranch compound went black. Lightning had probably taken out a transformer.

It was late. All in the other rooms of the bunkhouse were sound asleep. No one would notice the power outage.

But then she saw a lantern light from behind the stable. Someone was up, checking on the horses.

She rose from the rocker and pulled on her slicker. A walk to the stable would clear her head. She could check on Girlie, too. No doubt the poor animal was still frightened.

The stable door opened and closed as she approached. In the driving rain, she couldn't tell who was there. Secretly she hoped it was Justin. He was just so much easier to deal with.

Slipping inside the stable, she shut the battened door behind her and looked to the circle of yellow lantern light.

The silhouette of a man straightened. He was tall and muscular, a low-slung cowboy hat on his head.

"Couldn't sleep?" Bruce asked.

She shook her head and came forward. "I figured I'd check on Girlie. I was worried about her in the storm."

He raised the lantern and studied her in the flickering light. "Good thinking. Maybe you can hold the lantern while I get her hind leg out between the boards she kicked open."

"She's hurt?" Lyndie's heart quickened.

"If I can get her free, she might just be a little sore. But I'd sure hate to find out she's broken her hock, struggling against all those boards."

"No," she gasped, her hand over her mouth.

"You wanna help?" He held out the lantern.

"Anything. Anything at all," she offered, taking the lantern and going with him to Girlie's stall.

The palomino was in the corner of her stall, her right hind leg vised between the corner boards. With every new flicker of lightning, the animal would wrench her leg and violently toss her head.

"Talk to her. See if you can calm her, and I'll take care of the leg," he ordered.

She nodded, whispering softly to the frightened mare and stroking her sweat-covered neck.

"That's a girl," he murmured, and she wondered if he was talking to her or Girlie.

"Easy. Easy…" He took the animal's rear leg in a grip like a blacksmith getting ready to shoe her. Then, feeling for the rest of the appendage, he reached into the dark hole where she'd kicked off the board.

"She may jump when I do this. I'm warning you," he growled.

Lyndie said nothing. He needed light, and she was determined to stand and hold the lantern.

"Take one hand on her halter. That way you may distract her."

She did as she was told. Girlie seemed to calm the minute Lyndie resumed her soothing words.

Bruce took a crowbar and broke the board that wedged her leg into the wall.

The loud crack even startled Lyndie. Girlie

lurched forward. Just as she did, Bruce pulled her leg free.

"She's not standing on it, but there's no blood that I can see," Lyndie offered, desperate for the pretty mare to be all right.

Bruce took a long time massaging and stroking the mare's leg.

Lyndie watched, mesmerized at the contrast of strength and gentleness. His large hands could probably be capable of inflicting pain, and yet Girlie reacted to his touch as if she were a cat having her favorite owner scratch her.

Briefly, she recalled how his hands had felt on her at the mill. His touch commanded and seduced.

The man was dangerous…

Snapping out of her thoughts, she stepped back so he could lead Girlie by the halter out of her stall.

"She's fine!" she cried out when she saw the animal put weight on her rear leg.

"She'll probably be a little sore tomorrow. You can take another animal if we go out trail riding, but from what the weather service reports, I don't think anyone's going anywhere." He rubbed Girlie's nose with his knuckles.

"You're bleeding," she blurted before she could stop herself.

He looked down at his hand and the red smudge on Girlie's nose. "It's nothing. Just a few nicks from the board."

"Do you have a first-aid kit here? I could wrap it for you."

He chuckled. "The Panty Princess is a nurse, too? My, what talents you have, Miss Clay."

"Hey, I only offered to—"

He took her by the waist and pulled her to him. For a moment, he stared down at her, studying her every feature, seemingly trying to read her emotions from her face.

"What are you afraid of?"

"Afraid? I'm not afraid," she said.

"Yep. You're afraid, all right. You play all these little games with me and Hazel because it lets you avoid the real issue."

"Which is?" Her face flushed with newborn anger.

"That you're unwilling to take a chance. To have fun. You're afraid of liking it."

"I have lots of fun in New Orleans, believe me. It's 24/7 fun, fun, fun down there," she rattled on.

His undamaged knuckles ran down the smooth curve of her cheek. His every stroke was like a tongue of fire, licking lower and lower.

"Let loose, princess. I dare you," he whispered, just as his lips came down on hers.

She squeezed her eyes shut and devoured his kiss like a starving woman. It wasn't true what he'd said, but somehow she couldn't get the words out of her mind. Taking chances was too risky with a broken heart. She had nothing left to fracture.

But nonetheless, she opened her mouth for his searching tongue.

The kiss got hotter, and hotter still. His hand moved up from her waist. With a jolt of carnal electricity, she felt him cup her breast. He massaged her nipple through the fabric of her bra and shirt. It responded like all things feminine responded to him: wanting more.

"Have you ever made love to a man by lantern light? With all heaven and earth letting loose above?" he whispered, his voice melding with the drum of rain on the roof.

Girlie nickered, then stole a mouthful of hay from another horse's hay ball.

"Of course I've never done that. Adults don't do such things," she protested thickly, her words sounding drunk from his kiss.

"So tell me, what do adults do?" he taunted gently, his hand on her waist tightening, pulling her ever closer.

"They go to dinner. They have sex in a real bed with nice clean sheets and a nearby shower."

"Not talking about sex, girl. I'm talking about making love."

She stopped short. They were talking of two different things.

After Mitch, she could only imagine having sex

again, never making love. The latter required too much courage.

Bruce kissed her again, deeply. His lips went to her throat, and then to the part of her raincoat. He slipped in his hand. Then he lowered her to the corner where a mound of fresh straw was piled.

"I can't do this," she gasped, her words barely audible over the thundering of her heart.

"Why? Because you might feel something?" he demanded, lowering on top of her, his weight intimidating. "Because there's no hell on earth like living and not feeling?"

He stroked her face, then fingered her cleavage through the buttoned part of her shirt.

He was right, of course. She'd been living for months, numb and half-dead, her vitality killed by betrayal.

She moaned a surrender while he unbuttoned her shirt.

He took her nipple in his mouth through the fabric of her pink bra, wetting it. The sensation rolled through her like a drug.

Then, like a bath of cold water, the lights flashed on.

She lay on the hay looking up at him, mortified that she was barely in her bra, displayed beneath the harsh glare of a dozen fluorescent lights.

He glanced up at the lights, cursed under his breath, then rolled off her.

Adjusting himself, he helped her to her feet and picked the straw from her hair.

"Well, I call the winner of this round, I guess—" he said ruefully, as she fumbled with the buttons on her shirt.

"Winner? Of what?" she asked, not following him.

"The seduction game."

She looked up at him. His gaze taunted and dared.

"The game's not over," she whispered, before grabbing her raincoat and running to the safety of the bunkhouse.

Six

——

She hated him. The humiliation of Bruce's parting words was enough for Lyndie to decide that she really and truly hated him.

To make matters worse, she was trapped with him in the lodge during a day of continuous downpour.

While the others played cribbage and drank tea by the big fieldstone hearth, Lyndie sat off to one corner, playing solitaire on her laptop.

She really should pack it in, she told herself. Toying with a cowboy was a waste of time and energy. A road to nowhere—or worse.

And she didn't need the emotional torrents, either. There seemed no middle ground where Bruce was concerned. She either surrendered gladly, or fought with all her might. He seemed to inspire passion in her that knew no blandness, only fire and consummation.

But it wasn't love.

Love was comfort and security, not this terrible raw emotion that lay naked within her, as naked as she had felt when those fluorescent lights came on.

"Whatcha doing?" Susan asked, peering over the screen of Lyndie's laptop.

Embarrassed, Lyndie logged off and put the computer aside. "Nothing. Just work. Trying to catch up." As if she could do that, with all the turmoil within her.

Susan smiled. She was a tiny woman with straight mousy-brown hair and a preference for black clothing; very L.A. "I guess it's hard to keep up with work when you're busy chasing cowboys."

Lyndie stopped short. "Why would I be doing that?"

"You and Bruce Everett are the talk of the ranch." Susan gave her another gamine grin. "I have to admit, I'm wicked jealous."

"Well, surely— I mean, I don't— I mean, you don't have to be," Lyndie stammered. "Jealous, that is. There's nothing between Bruce and me. I only had to ride with him because my horse Girlie is afraid of lightning."

"My horse is as steady as this rain coming

down." Susan sighed. "You know, I've got a fab fiancé back in L.A. But I take one look at Bruce Everett, and I'm rethinking the whole thing."

"That would be a mistake. He's certainly handsome, I admit—"

"Handsome?" Susan exclaimed. "He's a Greek god in chaps."

For some strange reason, Lyndie nearly choked on her words. "Hey, if you're interested in him, then, go for it. I don't have any special hold on him."

"Really?" This time it was Susan's turn to seem dumbfounded.

"Really," Lyndie answered succinctly.

After all, what did she care what a woman from L.A. did with the big bad cowboy, she told herself, hoping the rationale would chase away the conflicted feeling inside her.

The feeling that, if she didn't know better, smacked of jealousy.

Lyndie looked up. Bruce had just entered the lodge. She gave him a dismissive glance, then added, "He's all yours." She rose from her seat and made to go.

Susan stared at her. "Gee, thanks," she said.

"No problem." Lyndie left without looking back.

The next morning dawned clear and cold. Lyndie was up early and went to see Girlie in the paddock.

As Bruce had predicted, the mare was sore—lame, to be exact—but there seemed no permanent damage.

"You want to take Heartthrob today?" Justin asked her as he dumped sweet feed into the horses' buckets.

Lyndie shrugged. "I was thinking I might take the day off with Girlie. I want to see Hazel and let her know I'll be leaving the ranch earlier than I thought."

"You will?" Justin seemed way too interested.

She shrugged. "Do you think I could get an evening ride with Girlie if she's up to it? I'd love to have one more trail with her."

"If she's sound by then, I don't know why not. It's up to Bruce, though. He says who comes and goes in this place."

"Well, he certainly doesn't have that authority over the guests." She smiled, trying to give herself a confidence she didn't quite feel.

"Yes, ma'am." Justin tipped his hat.

She gave Girlie one more rub on the nose and headed for her cabin.

Justin watched her go, then headed for the tack room phone.

"Hazel? This's Justin over at the dude ranch."

He listened, then got on with his business. "I got

some pretty interesting news for you. She's leaving early.''

He listened again, flinching at the curses coming from the earpiece.

''Yep. She'll be in her cabin all day.'' He nodded. Then nodded again.

Then he hung up.

The morning's trail ride hadn't even begun before Lyndie heard a commanding knock on her bunk-room door. Convinced it was Bruce trying to get her on a horse, she threw open the door, the admonish-ment ready on her lips.

But it wasn't Bruce. It was Hazel. The woman's expression was concerned and exasperated at the same time.

''What brings you out here, Hazel?'' Lyndie mo-tioned for her to enter her room.

''Heard tell you're leaving again, and I don't mind letting you know that you're making me feel like I'm chasing my tail here.''

Lyndie rubbed her eyes, which she knew were puffy and red from lack of sleep. ''It's no good, Hazel. I've tried relaxing—''

A thought just occurred to her. ''Hey,'' Lyndie exclaimed. ''How'd you know I wanted to leave early? Are you bugging the place? Or is everyone here your spy?''

''Now, smooth those feathers. You've been telling everyone here you'll be leavin' early, haven't you?'' Hazel took a seat in the rocker, making herself at home.

Lyndie conceded. "I suppose."

Hazel looked inexplicably relieved. "And what about our wager?" The cattle baroness tossed a glance behind her at the open door.

Beyond, Bruce and Susan were laughing over some shared joke before getting ready to ride with the rest of the trail group.

"Just some friendly old lady advice, my dear—I don't think you're trying hard enough to win the bet."

"Maybe Susan and Bruce are better suited. Besides, I tried to seduce him and it just didn't work. I'm better off spending what little energy I have working for Milady."

"Why do you fight it so hard?"

Hazel's words disarmed Lyndie. Without even being aware of them, tears slipped out of Lyndie's eyes and fell down her cheek.

Resignedly she sat on the edge of the bed. "I don't know, Hazel. When you've seen your world explode, you just can't relax anymore..."

"Nonsense. Your world's just peeking over the horizon. You just need a good man, a good snowstorm and a good bottle of wine. Believe me, you'll see worlds a-plenty that way."

Lyndie laughed through her tears. "If your matchmaking skills are that clichéd, Hazel, I'm surprised you crow about them so much.''

"I've had more than one couple unite in wedded bliss with just the man and the snowstorm.'' Hazel harumphed. She stood, and the rocker creaked back and forth, leaving Lyndie's nerves as raw as the floorboards.

"Only God can produce a snowstorm, love,'' Hazel began.

"And you're not God, Hazel,'' Lyndie finished.

Hazel smiled, the light back in her eyes. "Yes, but I'm the next best thing, and don't you forget it.''

Lyndie laughed again. It was good to release the tension.

"You've got a lot of life in you, Lyndie. And first I'm going to get you to relax, or I'll be a heifer in a whiteout.''

"A what?'' Lyndie widened her eyes.

"That's for ranchers to know.'' Hazel winked. "Now, looky here, I'll promise you no shenanigans, but then I'll have to have your promise to stay. Is that final?''

"I'll hang on for one week, then I must begin to get you your money back.'' Lyndie held her breath.

"One week. But here it's all play and *no work*, got it?''

"Got it. In fact, I think I did pretty well at the stomp Saturday night, don't you?''

Hazel chuckled. "You were all McCallum then,

dear. A few more days of that kind of behavior and if you aren't willing to stay after that, then nothing I do can help.''

Taking the older woman's hand, Lyndie squeezed it. ''Hazel, when did you become so reasonable?''

Hazel scowled. ''When I got thwarted by my own kin, that's when.''

Lyndie laughed until her stomach ached. She was even beginning to feel that the rest of the week might be halfway enjoyable.

That was, if a certain cowboy could be held at arm's length. And if she didn't melt again, and long for his callused palms on her face, on her back, on her...

She mentally shook herself. It was up to her. She had a week of ranch living, and she could make Bruce and herself stay out of each other's company. She would enjoy herself without him, even if it meant spending the next week locked in the bunk-house playing horseshoes.

Seven

Lyndie was determined to sow some wild oats. And if Bruce Everett wasn't the man to do it with, she was bound to find one in Montana—cowboy heaven.

Bar-hopping never had been her thing, but she'd convinced Susan and her sister, Kim, to venture forth with her that night to a rowdy little place called Katown.

Taking Girlie for a brief evening ride beforehand, she thought the mare was healing nicely. Justin concurred as he led the short trail ride.

Lyndie had wanted to know where Bruce was, but refrained from asking. She didn't care. Indeed, he was handsome, but her encounters with him were too volatile to handle right now.

A good barfly flirtation was what she needed. Something that didn't count and never would.

"I hear you gals are thinking of going to Katown." Justin mentioned on the way back to the barn.

"We're thinking of it." Lyndie patted Girlie on the neck.

"You ever been there?"

Lyndie shook her head. "Why?"

"Pretty rough crowd down there. Beginnin' of the last century, it used to be the red-light district for the mining operations this side of the Divide. Hazel's grandmother nearly burned the Katown bar to the ground trying to rid the place of vermin that might come crawling to Mystery."

"Sounds perfect," Lyndie announced.

"Bruce ain't gonna let you go alone. You know that, don't you?" Justin said.

"And what say does he have in the matter?"

"You gals are our guests. The guests are always right, but that don't mean we let 'em hitchhike out of the ranch. Somebody's got to get you there and that would be Bruce."

"Fine. I don't mind a chauffeur. I never have."

"He'll do more than drive you around, that's for sure. Even now, he can't barely let you out of his sight."

Lyndie gave him a strange glance. "What's that supposed to mean?"

Justin shrugged and his expression went purposefully blank. "Nothin'" was all he said, as they arrived at the paddock and gave the stable hand their mounts.

The ride to Katown was awkward. Lyndie took the third-row seat in the ranch's huge SUV, and Bruce drove. Justin, Susan and Kim filled in between. Still, the tension between Bruce and Lyndie was palpable.

Kim flirted with Justin. Susan chatted with Bruce in the front seat.

Lyndie wasn't sure, but she swore Bruce stared at her in the rearview mirror. As usual, she couldn't read his hard, inscrutable expression. Whether his thoughts were on her, she'd never know. All she did know was that with every passing day, he was getting more and more under her skin.

Tonight she was determined to exorcise him from her thoughts forever.

"I got to warn you gals." Justin spoke up. "Katown isn't the nicest of places. Most of the bars have the band behind a chain-link cage. It's been known to be a rough spot—"

"Do they have cowboys there?" Lyndie asked, recklessly.

Justin paused. "Mostly the kind that go there are either guys who work in the mines or they're ranch hands ready for a long drunk. Not too many cowboys, at least not the way you gals think of 'em.''

"But you're a real cowboy, aren't you?'' Kim asked, squeezing his hand.

"I was raised on a cattle ranch. And I was taught to treat ladies like ladies.'' Justin snorted. "But that don't mean much to the characters in Katown. They'll all tell you they're cowboys, just to get some.''

Lyndie began to wonder if her wild night out was such a good idea. But before she could mull it over further, they pulled onto a dirt road and entered the little crossroads nestled beneath the Bitterroot range.

Bruce parked the SUV. Justin helped Kim, Susan and Lyndie from the car.

Already they could hear men fighting in the saloon across from them called the Broke Spoke. There were more motorcycles out front than there were pickups.

"Let's not go inside and say we did,'' Susan said nervously.

"You all feel free to go back to the ranch,'' Lyndie announced. "I can always call a cab to take me home.''

Bruce looked almost angry. "Sure. But if we leave you here alone, you won't be needin' the cab. We may never find you again.''

Lyndie smiled. "Don't be silly. I can take care of myself.''

"I'd like to see you try."

Lyndie felt as if he'd just thrown down the gauntlet.

Susan looked nervous and clung to Bruce's arm.

As much as Lyndie denied it, the sight shot a stream of jealousy through her veins.

"Then, brace yourself," she taunted, then walked toward the entrance of a saloon called the Blue Bronc.

Smoke filled the dark saloon. Along with it came the smell of body odor and spilled beer.

A four-piece Western band played in the far corner. She was relieved to see it wasn't in a cage, but then, the band members looked more hairy and mean than even the clientele.

"What's your pleasure, beautiful?" the bartender asked as she sidled to the bar.

"Uh-h." Lyndie only knew she didn't want whiskey, that was for sure.

"She wants a whiskey!" a man called out from the end of the bar. He was a large man with a full black beard and a tattoo of the flaming-skull-and-rose kind.

"No, uh, really—" she protested before the whiskey was set before her.

"It's on Joe," the bartender told her as he pointed to the husky man at the end of the bar.

"Th-thank you." Lyndie tried to hide her grimace, but didn't think she was doing a very good job.

She must have been a more brilliant actress than she'd thought, because Joe came right up to her and put his arm around her.

"My, ain't you a pretty little thing. Where you from, sugar?" He smiled. His teeth were tobacco-stained but at least all there.

"I'm from New Orleans."

"New Orleans! They do some serious partyin' down there, now, don't they?"

Lyndie released a silent sigh of exasperation. If this was her wild night out to forget about Mitch and Bruce Everett, it was off to an unpromising start.

"Actually, all I do there is work. Work, work, work. All work and no play. Sorry."

She sipped from the whiskey glass, pacing herself.

He smiled his yellowed smile through the huge beard. "Glad to meetcha, little lady."

She didn't really care to speak to the lout, but in the mirror behind the bartender, she saw Bruce and the rest of the gang enter the bar. At all costs, she didn't want to let on that she was lost or scared.

Joe stared at her and took a long mouthful of whiskey. "So, what do you do down in New Orleans, little lady?"

She opened her mouth to reply, then thought better of it. There was no point in fanning Joe's flames with visions of silk panties and bras.

"I'm a schoolteacher. Uh—kindergarten."

That was pretty safe. She cringed at the lie, but it definitely seemed like the more prudent path.

"I never finished high school myself." He squeezed her.

She wondered how she was ever going to get his arm off her.

"How interesting."

"You've met a real-live mountain man—right, Ian?" He winked at the bartender.

"I live off the land, darlin'. I hunt and fish, and I got to tell you, sugar, you look pretty fine to a man who's been up in the mountains for a very long time."

She was speechless.

"What say you and I get a little closer?"

He swept his big hand down her back.

She swore he patted her rear, but since she wasn't sure, she didn't want to make a federal case of it.

"You mean you don't have women lining up to go live amongst the splendor of the mountains?" She hoped she'd hidden her cynicism.

"I don't want to talk about them. I want to talk about where you're stayin' tonight, darlin'." He hugged her again.

And this time, there was no mistaking the grip on her rear.

She tried to step away, but he snatched her to him.

Coldly, she said, "Hey look, I don't mind a little friendly chat, but I don't want to be mauled."

"Who's maulin' ya, huh? Not me, huh? I'm just a good ol' boy in town for a while, wanting a good ol' time." He bent to kiss her.

Her adrenaline surged.

Trying to push him away, she spat, "Look, you might be a legend in your own mind, but I'm not really impressed. So hands off!"

His eyes chilled with anger.

"You uppity woman. You come in here thinkin' you're too good for us, huh? Well, I'll give you a spin around tonight that'll put you in your place."

It wasn't quite a scream that came out of her mouth, it was more of a half moan, half grunt as she tried to shove the man away. She was just realizing she couldn't succeed, when someone pulled him off her.

"She said scat." Bruce, his face filled with unspent rage, nearly lifted Joe off his feet.

"Who are you?" Joe hollered.

"Nobody you need to know, just somebody you need to listen to," Bruce answered ominously.

Lyndie was ready for Joe's retort.

But not the fist that met with Bruce's eye.

Her instinct was to rush to Bruce's side to see if he was okay.

But she was completely out of her element. Bruce

ignored her cry of sympathy and laid several nasty blows in Joe's gut.

"Stop this!" she exclaimed, but neither of them listened. It was as if they were stags in rut, acting on nothing but testosterone and rage.

"Stop this at once!" she demanded, as Bruce laid into Joe like a madman.

Joe, bloody and aching, began to look afraid of the man he'd riled.

"Please stop!" she screamed, before any other men could join in the fray.

Bruce withheld the final blow and Joe sank against the wall.

"I can't believe this," she gasped, staring at Bruce.

"Well, believe it," he said, fury snapping in his cold eyes. "You got what you wanted. We came here. Now we're leaving."

"I didn't want this! I wanted a night out." She looked around.

Justin was holding Kim and Susan by the arm as if comforting both of them.

Everyone in the bar was staring at her and Bruce.

"Maybe your boyfriend's right, lady. Maybe you ought to leave," the bartender nudged.

Bruce grabbed her by the hand. He pulled her out of the bar and toward the SUV.

"Believe me," she implored, "I never thought

something like this would happen. I mean, I can take care of myself—''

He stopped in his tracks and stared at her.

She suddenly felt as foolish as she probably looked. "I'm sorry. Maybe I couldn't take care of myself back there. I guess I should admit it and thank you."

"I don't want your thanks," he sniped.

"Then, what do you want? An apology? Look, I'm sorry, but I had no idea that would happen, and I certainly didn't plan on getting you a black eye this evening."

"I don't want your apology."

She looked at him, defeated. "Then, what do you want? My blood? What else is there?"

"This—"

He grasped her chin and tilted her head up toward him. His lips planted on hers in a deep yearning kiss.

"Whewwweee!"

The voice made them freeze.

Lyndie stepped away from Bruce, only to find Justin, Susan and Kim staring at her.

She flushed with embarrassment—and guilt.

Susan had been quite clear she wanted to go for Bruce, and Lyndie had made it clear she wasn't interested. At best, she now looked like a hypocrite, at worst, like a liar.

"This—this isn't what it looks like," she stammered, trying to inject some sense into the insane night.

"It looked pretty clear to me," Justin remarked.

"Me, too," Susan said softly.

"Everyone get in the truck. We're going back to the ranch," Bruce ordered gruffly, glancing at her as if she'd somehow betrayed him, too.

Resigned to an even more tense ride back to the ranch, Lyndie got in the car, but found her seat taken by Susan. With Kim and Justin in the middle seat, she had no choice but to sit up front with Bruce.

She slid into the truck, confused and chagrinned.

She desperately wanted to talk her way out of the situation, but she couldn't, when all had witnessed what was crystal clear. She and Bruce had been kissing and it hadn't been their first kiss. And even if she could lie to him, she could no longer lie to herself.

She had let him kiss her. She had wanted him to kiss her.

Twisting her lips in a wry grin, she tried to think of something humorous to say that might make the ride back a little more tolerable.

But it was no use. She didn't utter a sound. Nor did Bruce before he sped out of Katown as if a posse were after them.

Eight

The rain started about midnight. Lyndie knew it because they'd been back at the ranch for almost an hour.

Bruce had unceremoniously left the group at the bunkhouse and gone to park the SUV in the ranch's garage. She didn't see him again, though his light was on in his cabin.

Cold droplets sprayed on her face as she rocked on the porch and studied the thin yellow glow coming from beneath his door. The cabin was over a hundred yards away and looked even farther in the falling mist.

Emotionally, she believed the cabin was in another universe, where honesty and bravery ruled, not in her universe where she was wounded and afraid.

She wanted to hate him. Bruce Everett represented everything Mitch had done to her. His swagger and easy seductive manner was very similar to Mitch's, and it frightened her.

Instead of being an adult and telling Bruce she wasn't up to a flirtation with him right now, she wanted to play games, and kiss him. And run away.

Adults didn't behave this way, she admonished herself.

But the hurt little girl in her kept crying.

She needed to apologize to him. He'd protected her when all she'd done was amuse herself at his expense. In fact, that's all she'd done since she'd arrived at Mystery.

In the distance, a flood of yellow light illuminated the rain.

Lyndie looked up and found Bruce's silhouette standing in the open door to his cabin.

Her knee-jerk reaction was to stand, as if readying for…

A thrill wove down her back as she watched him walk toward her in the dark and the rain. The icy sting of the rain pelted her face, but she hardly noticed. All she saw was him, walking to her. All she heard was the primal drum of rain on boards.

She watched as he came ever nearer, his shadowed form growing larger and more ominous with every step.

Finally, when he was close enough to see her, he stood in his tracks, rain-sodden and tense, staring, as if she were prey.

"I *am* sorry." She half swallowed her words. Her throat was choked with some unnamed emotion.

"I didn't come for an apology." His words were harsh.

He came no nearer. He had to wipe the rain from his face.

"Then, why did you come?" she asked in a hushed voice. But her question was rhetorical. She knew.

"From the day I laid eyes on you, something came alive inside me. Something I thought was dead. That night at the mill, I knew I wanted you. I haven't thought about much else since."

She took in what he was saying like a beggar, and she hated herself for it. Her reaction to him proved she was susceptible game. There was no longer any need to protect herself, because he'd won. He'd made her recognize her need. She was still alive inside, too. She was still a woman. His last conquest would be to make her need him and him alone.

Numb and yet strangely giddy, she drew back and opened her bunkhouse door.

The light inside spilled onto the porch, onto him.

He stared at her in the rain, his jeans soaked, his

T-shirt clinging like transparent film. He was tall and muscular, harsh, and yet gentle.

Her attraction to him was uncontainable. And she no longer wanted to try to contain it.

Slowly she walked in through the bunkhouse door, leaving it open.

He followed her. The last of the outside world was shut away when she heard him close the door, then lean against it, as if barricading them in with his back.

Minutes seemed to pass as Lyndie stared at the wet man in front of her.

Bruce had to be cold, she thought, but he didn't shiver. He just studied her back, until suddenly he reached for her, and she let him, unmindful of the wetness, blank to any sensation that was not the pure, warm, dark essence of male.

He kissed her.

His mouth took, his tongue probed.

Her lips thrummed with desire for his taste, his demands.

She felt drugged as he broke from her to slip out of his T-shirt. Now she could see what she could not at the mill.

His chest was smoothly rippled, finely sprinkled with black hair. Steel beneath velvet.

She couldn't stop her hand from resting there, to see if he felt as erotic as he looked.

She was not disappointed.

The warmth on her hand spread to her belly and then to her thighs. Her emptiness became unbearable. She wanted him, on top of her, covering her, inside her. She wanted him all night and maybe the next and the next one after that. Her hunger was insatiable.

His hand went to her nape and pulled her to him.

Without speaking, he kissed her again, this time unbuttoning his soaked jeans and forcing her hands to the waistband so she could help pull them off.

She moaned when he unzipped her fleece jacket. She was still in the silk camisole and tap pants that she slept in. To go out to the porch, all she'd done was slip into her jacket and pull on a pair of jeans.

He seemed pleased by the easy access. He made quick work of the jacket, then slipped his hand beneath the shimmering pale pink silk.

Her resistance crumbled.

Perhaps it was partly the callused palm on her breast, or the surprising warmth of his mouth on her nipple.

But in the end, it was his scent. While Mitch had smelled of expensive cologne and starch, Bruce smelled of rain and the darker scent of aroused male.

There was only one way to purge both their systems of this strange attraction.

They were so different, she thought, and yet as he sat on the edge of the bed and pulled her to him, nothing seemed more natural, more comfortable. His hands gave her assurance and warmth, even when the last of her clothing was gone. His words kept her mind on the moment and her need, blessedly away from everything rational and prudent.

Finally with a last soul-searching kiss, he lowered his body to hers.

He was naked, hard and hot, and she wanted him like an alcoholic wants a drink. Her thirst became insatiable, even destructive, but she didn't care.

He parted her thighs with his hand and thrust himself inside her. His breath quickened; she moaned. The fullness was ecstasy. She didn't ever want him to leave.

She reached up to his chest and felt the hammer of his heartbeat begin to meld into the rhythm of his lovemaking. His tense, muscular legs rocked against her womanly soft thighs. Then he grew more fierce and demanding, and her body went with him, finally building into a long, racking release.

The fall was exquisite.

She took her orgasm and held it inside until tears filled her closed eyes. The feeling was life-affirming, yet terrifying; satiating, yet agonizing—taunting her that there might be no more.

He stared down at her. She clutched him to her though his back was slick with sweat.

Finally, when he could take no more, he devoured her mouth in a searing kiss and spilled himself inside her. His release racked his torso with pleasure, his muscles steeled with barely contained strength.

The silence afterward should have horrified her. Instead, it was like a blanket of peace that lulled her into sleep.

Her last thought as she snuggled within his arms was that she could get used to sleeping this way, protected in his strong embrace, serenaded by the rain falling on the shake roof.

Waking the next morning was the hardest thing Lyndie ever had to do. Sunlight spilled through the bandana curtains of her bunkroom, her bedside lamp was still on. Next to her, the sheets were cold and empty.

It seemed the dream, like a fire, had turned to ashes.

She took a deep cleansing breath and tried to summon her courage.

She didn't know how to go about the day. She was not the kind to act on an impulse, but last night had been just that. She was lonely and Bruce had offered comfort. She'd thrown good sense to the wind and had taken everything he'd offered.

Now she had to deal with it, no matter how painful, no matter how awkward and humiliating.

As she saw it, she had two options: she could pretend last night never happened and go breezily about her way at the ranch, or she could admit to the intimacy they'd shared last night and hope he reciprocated the goodwill.

She moaned and wished she were anywhere but there. New Orleans suddenly seemed so safe and secure. Even Mitch didn't seem to matter as much as he had before. Now all she could think about was Bruce Everett. And what to do about him. And how to save herself.

Outside she heard Justin ring the bell to saddle up. She'd missed breakfast, but that wasn't much of a sacrifice these days. She hadn't much appetite, anyway.

Forcing herself out of the bed, she slipped on a bra and panties, grateful there wasn't time for a shower. The scent on her body was too delicious to wash away.

She threw on her riding jeans and a white oxford shirt and walked out her door, bracing herself for whatever came her way.

"There she is. Girlie's all tacked up and waitin' for you." Justin greeted her with a smile.

Looking around for Bruce, she didn't find him among the mounted riders. Susan gave her a rather baleful stare, but Kim seemed all too pleased to be riding in front, right behind Justin.

"Where's our fearless leader?" Roger thankfully exclaimed as they headed out of the paddock.

"He's off on his own this morning. Headed out

before dawn. He'll catch up to us. Always does,'' Justin called out.

Lyndie was thankful she hadn't had to ask, but she was still tortured by questions. She wondered why Bruce had gone off on his own and where, but when they reached the fork in the trail, she looked up the forbidden path and saw fresh hoofprints in the mud.

It answered a lot of questions.

Suddenly chilled, she wrapped herself in her fleece jacket and tried to concentrate on what Justin was lecturing ahead about soapberries and the grizzlies that loved to eat them.

It was no use.

Her mind was filled with the vision of Bruce and Beastie Boy standing on the cliff that had taken Katherine.

She suddenly feared last night had been a mistake. She had had no business getting herself involved with a man who was still mourning. There was little future for her with him, anyway. He was a dyed-in-the-wool good ol' boy from Montana, and she was a career-minded businesswoman from the French Quarter. They were worlds apart. They were oil and water.

"My, you're quiet this morning, lovey," Annette tsked. "Did the trip last night give you a head?"

Lyndie thought she knew what the woman meant. "You mean a hangover?"

Annette smiled at Roger knowingly.

Lyndie smiled when she wanted to cry. "No, I haven't got a hangover. We didn't do much drinking last night, after all."

"Home in bed early. That's how I like my nights," Roger commented pleasantly.

"Yes. Home in bed early," Lyndie repeated, her words fading with the hope in her heart.

Nine

Lyndie wasn't ready to face what had happened the night before. Her rash and impulsive jump into bed with Bruce still left her breathless. Confused and shaken, she had just finished an afternoon cup of coffee in the lodge when Susan sat down next to her, a frown on her face.

"I have to tell you," Susan began, "I don't appreciate you making a fool out of me in front of Bruce. You knew all the time I was confessing to you that you were involved with him, and yet you let me continue talking. I hope you had a good laugh."

Lyndie shook her head, her cheeks red with chagrin. "We weren't involved. Really. That kiss just happened. It just happened."

"Sure. Well, let me tell you, you're either lying to me, or lying to yourself, because what I saw last night didn't just happen. Good afternoon to you, Lyndie."

Susan got up and left.

Watching her go, Lyndie realized the woman was right about one thing. The truth came at her like a freight train: she was lying to herself. It was ridiculous to think she could handle a man like Bruce. He was too independent and ferocious. And right now, she was too vulnerable.

Chair legs scraped on the floor.

Bruce sat next to her at the lodge table and stared, his legs stretched out before him, his arms crossed over his chest. His expression was stony, his black eye making him look vaguely pirate-like.

"That's some shiner," she said, desperate to keep the tone between them casual.

His mouth twisted in a grin. "You know the old line, don't you— You shoulda seen the other guy."

She smiled, though inside she wanted to flee.

"Sleep well last night?" he asked.

Her cheeks heated as she recalled the many times they'd made love. Even now, with him near, she wanted him, covering her, intoxicating her.

"It's hard not to sleep well after the workout you gave me."

She tried to keep it light, even though the night with him was the most earth-shattering encounter she'd ever had. No other man would ever live up to him—of that she was acutely, sorrowfully, aware. But it would do her no good to show weakness. He'd cut and run then, and she wouldn't even be able to blame him.

"It's been a while," he confessed, studying her.

"Insatiable. I think that's the word." She tried to laugh. It sounded flat even to her. Her gaze met his, and she was caught.

He demanded the truth, and she decided to give it a shot, especially since she was becoming terribly afraid of her feelings for him.

"I—I hope it was more than just playing catch-up," she stammered, hating to appear vulnerable after what had happened with Mitch.

"It was more than a roll in the hay."

Becoming unnerved by his stare, she looked away from him, desperate to cover herself, to hide.

"You should open a shop in Mystery, you know that," he said. "We get a lot of tourists either skiing or summering here. They'd keep you silky satin, all right."

She shrugged, helpless. "I can barely get my feet wet with two shops. How am I going to run a business here from New Orleans?"

"You got it all wrong. You need to run your New Orleans business from here." His expression grew taut with unexpressed emotion. "Believe me, I'll never tell you how to run your business, but you need to expand—"

"I'm planning to expand. That's why I got Hazel to invest. But I've got to pay her back, and soon." Her problems seemed to grow like a tsunami and overtake her. His words sounded wonderful, but she couldn't see her way out of the financial maze in which she was trapped. More than that, there had to be a bigger reason to move to Montana than money. She'd do it for love. But never for money.

"I can't see me being able to afford a third shop here, when I'm barely able to carry two stores on my shoulders. The numbers just won't work." She couldn't get around the fact that the only way to take on risk was with support—but all alone, jeopardizing everything, there was no way. Moving to Mystery could spell ruination for the shop.

A strange anger crackled in his eyes. "I ain't one to push the point with a lady, but I know more about business than you think. I think the numbers would work fine."

Her sigh seemed to echo through every timbered corner of the large lodge room. She didn't want to fight with him, especially over such dry matters. What she really wanted was for him to hold her hand and take her back to bed with him. She'd give anything to shut out the world just a little longer.

Defeated, she said, "I appreciate your input, but

it's my business and no one else's. I have to do what I think best. And it's best I return home to New Orleans.''

He stood, his face taut. ''You may come to regret that hasty conclusion, darling. There's nothing in New Orleans.''

Her head pounded from an oncoming headache. She couldn't figure out why their conversations always went wrong. ''Really?'' she asked. ''And how would you know? And what does Mystery have to offer?''

His eyes narrowed. ''You know what? I just figured you out. You're uppity just like Katherine was. A hardworking man isn't good enough for you. You want tuxedos and champagne when whiskey and jeans might serve you better.''

''Oh, let's not discuss whiskey...'' she begged.

He became silent.

Eventually he said, ''All I know is that I'm through paying stud service to your type. Next time, little lady, you want a workout, you'll be in my bed servicing me.''

He gave her one last deadly glance, then stormed out of the lodge, his hat pulled low over his angry eyes.

She stared at the closed door for what felt like a long, numbing moment.

Deep down she felt guilty, even sorrowful. And

she couldn't shake the feeling she'd lost something she'd never even known she had.

"Lookout Mountain's the first overnight trip we'll be taking." Justin turned the carousel of the slide projector. He was lecturing the group in the lodge after breakfast.

The morning had dawned with a crystal-blue sky and warm sun. Even Lyndie was anxious to go for a ride on Girlie and go find the day for herself.

"This," Justin explained, "is the terrain. As you can see, the drops are pretty magnificent. We just ask that you remain alert and let your horse guide you. Our animals are well-schooled in these mountains. Their instincts are good."

Lyndie watched the slide show with only half attention. The scenery was beautiful; the trail should be one of the best they'd been on. Still, she couldn't help feeling a sense of dread knowing she'd be camping overnight with Bruce.

"We're a little concerned," Roger piped up behind her. "We heard a woman was killed on one of those trails."

Justin grimaced. Even Lyndie was glad Bruce was not among the group to hear Roger's question.

"The woman was killed because she did not listen to her horse. We ask you to listen to what your mount is telling you. You won't have any trouble then." He turned grim. "Nonetheless, we won't be going on the trail where Katherine was killed, so no one need worry.''

"Is it the one we never take going out to the Divide?" Kim asked.

Justin nodded. "It's off-limits. Now you know why."

A murmur went through the small group. Several cowhands who were there to answer any questions shot one another an uncomfortable look.

They were glad, too, that Bruce wasn't there, Lyndie mused, knowing firsthand what a temper their boss had.

"Just 'cause we're going out on the trail don't mean you'll suffer." Justin continued with the slide show. "Horse-packers will go on ahead with all our gear and food. At the end of the trail, your dinner will be ready, your tent set up and your sleeping bag unrolled."

"What? No Jacuzzi for our saddle-sore muscles?" Annette added.

Justin laughed. "We do the best we can, ma'am. We can't have a Jacuzzi, but we have a coffee can with holes in it and a large piece of canvas. If you don't mind one of us standing over you pouring the warm water, you can even take a shower."

"Oh dear," Annette gasped.

"She'll bloody pass, she will," Roger proclaimed, putting a possessive arm over his plump wife.

This time even Lyndie joined in the laughter.

But her smile froze when her gaze found Bruce. He must have just walked in.

He stared at Lyndie as if there was something still unspoken between them.

"This morning's free time," Bruce announced. "Lyndie's great-aunt, Hazel McCallum, has been good enough to open her ranch to us this morning for a tour. Anyone who wants to go, see Justin."

The meeting was adjourned.

While the rest of the group went with Justin to the Lazy M, Lyndie decided to remain behind. She'd seen enough of the ranch on her own over the years, and she wasn't in the mood to share Hazel. Not when she needed a good heart-to-heart with her, instead.

Frustrated that she couldn't get on Girlie without a guide to accompany her, Lyndie decided to enjoy the morning on foot.

Pulling on her hiking boots, she took the usual path up the mountain. She'd gone several miles before she noticed she was on the path that forked. The terrain looked different on foot than from the back of a horse, but when she passed through a familiar glade of aspens, she found the split in the path straight ahead.

She could be more cautious walking than on a horse, she supposed. Perhaps it wasn't so dangerous, to go exploring as long as one didn't have to deal with the temperament of an animal.

Her feet seemed to make the decision for her. She climbed the near-vertical path until the fork was behind her, and then out of sight.

Compelled somehow to see the spot where Katherine died, and to see where Bruce went when he needed to be alone, she kept climbing, the view of the Divide getting more and more breathtaking with each step.

Finally, she reached a widening of the path. There was a ledge that looked out at the blue tops of the Rockies. She went to the edge. The drop was easily a hundred feet. No one could survive the fall.

But the panorama of mountains and sky was heaven meeting earth.

She stood there for a long time, hating to leave the solitude of the aerie. A peace flowed over her like the breeze that sang through the aspens below.

She turned, only to find herself looking at the furious expression on the face of Bruce Everett.

"The first rule of the wilderness is don't go anywhere alone," he snapped, dismounting Beastie Boy.

"I-I'm sorry," she stammered, rattled by his stealth.

"If something happened out here, who would know? Where would you get help?"

"I didn't think. I just wanted to see what was up

here. I figured walking would be safer than going on Girlie.''

''There's no difference. You still could have been hurt and no one would know where you were.'' He stepped toward her. ''Never do that again. Do you hear me?''

She nodded, his anger bringing tears to her eyes.

He had every right, she supposed, to chastise her. After all, he was in charge of the ranch's guests, and he was doubly responsible for her because she was Hazel McCallum's grand-niece.

''I guess curiosity got the best of me. I know we were told not to go anywhere alone, but I wanted to see where you—''

She hardly recognized the garbled cry in her throat.

Under the heels of her hiking boots, the ground was giving way. Somehow she must have misjudged the strength of the ledge and it was crumbling beneath her.

Paralyzed by fear, she realized Bruce's stricken face, and wondered if that was the last thing she would see before she, too, fell to her death.

''Do as I say. Take my hand,'' he commanded, dropping and sliding to her on his belly as if they were both on thin ice rather than thin ground.

She realized he'd tied Beastie Boy's reins to his chaps. That way, if they both fell, maybe the horse would be able to drag them to safety.

With a shudder of terror, she grabbed his hand.

He held on to her while the ground gave way beneath her, inch by agonizing inch.

The ledge was so fragile, she didn't dare move for fear of causing a larger piece to take them both down.

"You're okay. Everything's gonna be okay," he soothed in his deep familiar voice.

He barked a command to Beastie Boy and the animal began backing down the trail.

The ledge disappeared beneath her.

She screamed and felt the earth fall away from her scrambling legs.

One violent tug on her arm and she was yanked back onto the firm side of the trail. Beastie Boy dragged them several feet more before he halted.

In shock, she stared at Bruce. He faced her. They were both belly-down. The dust that had been kicked up as they were dragged stung her eyes.

"Thank you," she whispered, hardly able to breathe.

"You were a damn fool to come up here when we told you it was off-limits," he growled.

"Thank you," she rasped like an idiot, still unaware of anything around her except the fact that she was alive, and he had saved her.

"If I was the beatin' sort, I'd beat you silly, woman," he barked.

"Thank you," she said, starting to weep. "You

saved me. You saved me,'' she repeated again and again.

He got to his feet and reached to pull her to hers.

Only then did she feel the pain in her arm. She winced and pulled back.

He put his arm around her waist and helped her up. "You probably got it torn out of the socket," he said.

Weakly, she allowed him to put her on Beastie Boy, and together they rode down the mountain.

To ease her pain she found herself snuggling against his hard chest, as if to bury herself there. In just a few short seconds, everything in her life had changed, especially her feelings about the man who held her. He no longer seemed countrified and unworldly. Now he was a giant to her. A rescuer. A hero. Never again would she feel as safe as within this man's arms.

And all she could do was whisper her thanks to him, over and over again.

Ten

"**S**he's going to be a bit groggy. We gave her something for the pain, but you can take her home. Her arm should be sore for a couple of days, but nothing too bad. If she wants to go riding tomorrow, she can."

The emergency room doctor checked boxes off the sheet on his clipboard and gave the male nurse the okay to help Lyndie from the examining table.

"Thank you, Doctor," Hazel said, nodding.

Lyndie walked on her own to the ranch's SUV, refusing Bruce's strong arm. "We shouldn't have called you, Hazel. I'm fine," she said, embarrassed even in spite of all the painkillers.

"Nonsense," the cattle baroness huffed. "You sure you don't want to come to the Lazy M and recuperate?" Hazel asked.

"No, no. I'm fine. I'll go back to the dude ranch. Just a sore arm." Lyndie was adamant.

"Thank God you *are* fine. The way Bruce told it, you were in a pretty good scrape up there on the mountain, and believe me, he's Montana born and bred. He never exaggerates. Doesn't have to," Hazel added smartly.

Lyndie couldn't even look at Bruce. Her feelings were too raw and confused. "He saved me. I'm still trying to understand all that happened," Lyndie said, her words slurring from the medication.

"You get a good night's rest. You hear me, young lady? And no more shenanigans!" With a harumph, Hazel went to her Fleetwood in the parking lot.

Lyndie was placed by Bruce in the SUV.

"She's mad at me. You're mad at me," Lyndie said as they pulled out of the hospital pick-up zone. "And you both have every right to be. I had no business being up on that mountain."

Through the fog of painkiller, she still knew what she had to say. "I can never thank you enough for saving my life."

"I don't want you to say it again. You're not the first one to get in trouble up in the mountains and you won't be the last. It comes with the territory."

"I almost got you killed, too," she said, her voice shaky with tears. The horror was still too near.

"You are one helluva woman, Miss Clay. In the few short days I've known you, I've got a black eye, a scraped belly, and enough bullshit shoveled at me to last a lifetime."

He turned onto the highway and headed for the Mystery Dude Ranch. "Now, if you don't mind, I'd like to never hear the words 'I'm sorry' out of your mouth again."

"Okay. Sor—" She put her hand to her mouth.

She thought he pretended not to hear the mistake, and she was grateful. The day had already been too much for her. She couldn't think straight anymore. All she wanted was her bed and blessed sleep.

They turned onto the ranch. The bunkhouse came into sight. She could almost feel her muscles relaxing at the thought of her bed.

He stopped the SUV and helped her out and over to the bunkhouse. Throwing open her door, she looked at the bed, still rumpled from their lovemaking.

The remembrance made her flush.

"Do you want to come in?" she asked, turning around to face Bruce.

But no one was there.

Bruce was already in the SUV, barreling out of the ranch to parts unknown. And Lyndie hadn't the strength to follow.

* * *

Later that night, Hazel slid onto the tooled leather bar stool. She looked at the man next to her, hunkered down over his whiskey.

"Katherine's put to rest, son," she said, motioning to the bartender for another round.

Bruce looked down at his glass and swirled the gold liquid. "I know, Hazel, but I'm thinkin' I've had too much. When Lyndie almost died up there on that mountain, something inside me broke. I don't think I can take another woman in my life."

"Prowling around town for the rest of your life isn't the answer. At some point a man needs one woman. To raise a family. To have a home. You've had a nasty spell of bad luck, Bruce, but saving Lyndie changed that, don't you see?"

"All it changed was me," he snarled. "Lyndie's sure gotten under my skin, but I won't go through losing her like I lost Katherine. And the only way to guarantee that is to stay away. I can't lose what I don't have."

"Saving Lyndie was the remedy for all that guilt you've been holding on to, don't you see that?" Hazel implored.

"The only thing I see is this whiskey glass in front of me, old gal. And the only thing I'm going to feel is the thighs of the next woman I bed down with. And then the next woman after that, and after that."

Hazel stared at him, frustration lining her handsome face. She shoved her whiskey back to the bartender and slid from the stool. "I've never had to admit defeat before, son, but you're buckin' me off good this time. I can't force you to see when you're pigheaded stubborn about being blind."

She walked to the door and took one last look back at him.

"You got a lot going for you, Bruce Everett. Don't screw it all up out of fear. We all get hurt." With that, she left the saloon, and minutes later sped away in her cinnamon-and-black Fleetwood.

Lyndie didn't see Bruce again for two days. She and the rest of the dude ranch guests were well into the hills heading toward Lookout Mountain when they saw him on the trail coming toward them. He'd led the horse-packers that were to go ahead and set up camp. Then he'd headed back ready to lead them to camp. When the two parties met, there were hoots and hollers. Justin took a ribbing from the other cowboys when Bruce picked him to head the pack train, instead.

Bruce took the lead of their party. With hardly a nod to Lyndie, he headed them out toward the Divide and the jagged peak of Lookout Mountain.

Stunned that after all they'd been through he was now dealing her the cold shoulder, she tried and tried to make conversation with him, but there was no engaging him.

After lunch Susan took the second place in the line, and Lyndie volunteered to go to the rear.

He seemed to reanimate then. He and Susan shared a laugh when a jackrabbit shot out from the chaparral scrub and scurried away like a shot.

Behind them, Lyndie watched in misery. Her arm ached. In fact, her body was sore, but nothing matched the pain inside when she realized how far she had fallen for Bruce, and how cold he was being to her now.

They arrived at the Lookout campsite well before dusk. From the ridge, the entire Rockies seemed to lay out before them, snowtops beckoning like ice cream in summer.

The wind cut right through Lyndie. They were camping above the tree line, and though it was June in Mystery Valley, up high in the mountains it was subarctic summer.

A few flakes of snow began to fall when the chuck wagon was set up and the steaks were set to sizzling on the grill. Lyndie's tent already had a shimmering dust of white on the chartreuse nylon. All it needed was a red wreath, she thought, and it would feel like Christmas.

Dinner was quiet. The cowhands kept to themselves. She didn't even see Bruce. Roger and Annette retired to their tent early, claiming fatigue.

Only Susan and Kim stayed by the campfire with Justin, drinking a bottle of red wine. Their laughter grated on her.

Lyndie stood and said good-night. In her tent was a paperback thriller by her favorite author, Robert Ruthven. She figured that and a flashlight was better company than the resounding playfulness of the campfire group.

Walking to her tent, she spied the silhouette of a cowboy high on the face of the mountain. He was sitting by his own tent and campfire, moodily staring into the flames.

Bruce.

She studied him for a moment, unsure of how to approach him. There was a lot she wanted to say—but could she get out the right words?

Slowly, she climbed the basalt incline.

He looked up and watched her approach.

"I-I'm leaving tomorrow," she panted, out of breath from the exertion. "I just wanted to tell you."

Not moving, he stared at her from beneath the brim of his cowboy hat.

"You got my butt out of a pretty bad situation that I stupidly got into. I'll remember you. In many ways—" Her voice clogged with unexpected tears.

"Sit down," he commanded.

She did as she was told, facing him from the other side of the campfire.

"Hungry?" he asked.

Shrugging, she watched him cook a chunk of steak on the end of a stick. When it was almost black, he leaned over to hand it to her.

She took the stick but it was heavier than it looked. Her arm was too sore to lift it, and it fell in the fire.

"I ruined it!" she lamented.

"There's more. Tomorrow the coyotes will thank you." He watched her. "Your arm still sore, huh?"

She nodded.

"Won't do you much good with luggage, I expect."

"That's what porters are for. I've been a single woman traveling alone enough to know to carry lots of small bills." She smiled, desperate that their last moments not be ones of reproof.

"Make sure somebody lets me know how the session ended." She rubbed her aching hand. "I'll be thinking about you all. Wondering how things turned out."

"Everything will be jim-dandy. Don't worry."

"Oh, believe me, I'm not worrying." She released a tremulous smile. His chilled tone cut into her more deeply than she wanted to admit. "I know better than anyone else how capable you are."

She rambled, hoping mindless talk might take away some of the hurt. "I guess I just want to know if Roger and Annette really buy a pair of horses of their own as they said they want to. I want to know if Justin and Kim keep seeing each other after she goes back to L.A. Susan, I guess, too—'' she fought to continue ''—I want to know what happens to her. She's a great gal.''

"Yes."

He'd uttered one little word and suddenly she felt alone and unwanted. Not letting him see her tears, she stood and held out her hand.

"Goodbye, if I don't see you tomorrow."

He stood. In the flickering firelight, his face was shadowed, his expression unreadable.

"We're not ending this way," he rasped. "Not with a handshake, that's for sure."

"Then, what way?" she asked, desperate to leave so he wouldn't see her cry.

"This way."

He took her by the hand and led her to his tent.

Standing at the flap, he placed both hands on her face and gave her a long, sensual kiss. She moaned, wanting more, but afraid to fan the flames again, afraid of the pain and loneliness of tomorrow.

"This doesn't make it easy to say goodbye," she almost sobbed when he broke from her.

"Don't think about the goodbye, then."

He pulled her to her knees and followed her into the tent.

Outside the fire crackled and drew shadows along the orange nylon of the tent. Inside, he covered her with his body and drew his tongue along the sensitive hollow of her neck.

"I can't stay here," she begged, as he brushed away her tears and kissed the trails they'd left on her cheeks.

"It's cold up here. Stay and be warm."

She watched him strip out of his polar fleece jacket and jeans.

She knew if she stayed there, her heart would pay the price. But snuggled in the soft warmth of his down sleeping bag, the last place she wanted to be was outside or alone in her tent.

He leaned over her, his hard naked body reacting like a coiled spring ready for the release of lovemaking.

With silent questions, his hands went to her clothing. She gave silent answers as he tugged it off, piece by piece. Only once did she wince, when her arm had to be raised to slip off her shirt. He tossed the shirt aside, then kissed her arm, languorously tonguing each fingerprint bruise he'd made as he'd pulled her to safety.

"Is this wrong?" she asked when he covered them both with his sleeping bag.

He never answered her; he didn't need to.

Instead his tongue explored her mouth, then lower until he tasted her, licking her as if she was filled with honey. A long, sweet feeling of ecstasy gripped her until she had her hands wrapped around his head, begging him for more.

He lifted to kiss her mouth, mingling their essences to make only one—one that was uniquely theirs.

Hot and aroused, his shaft was like a brand against her belly, teasing her, forcing her to want more and more, until she was lost to him, she feared, forever.

The loveplay began in earnest when he coerced her to straddle him and allow his hands to cup her full breasts. He filled her to gasping, and he groaned his encouragement to ride him as fast and furious as a mustang.

Their pleasure came sharply, unexpectedly. First hers, in a slow, showering melt that weakened her and made her fall against his chest. Then his, in a sharp spasm, his hands gripping her hips as if to pull himself inside her and never let go.

Eventually, she felt his muscles relax between her tender thighs. The afterglow settled like snowflakes, until, insatiable, he reached for her half in slumber. He whispered love words. She moaned her approval. Without allowing the world to intrude, they began the dance all over again.

Eleven

"**I**'m in love with him." Lyndie gave Hazel the grim news as Hazel drove her to the airport.

"I'm in love with him, and for what? For nothing," Lyndie recounted bitterly as the miles dropped behind the Caddy.

"Lyndie dear, I've always told my gals that you've got to have a backbone and not a wishbone." Hazel studied her, then looked back at the road. "But in your case, gal, I'll take the wishbone. A leap of faith might do you good."

Lyndie shrank back in the seat and rubbed her aching arm. "He didn't even say goodbye. We broke camp and I never saw him again."

"He didn't want you to go. He was probably sore about it."

Rolling her eyes, Lyndie watched the deep summer green that rode the valley. Her retort was irrefutable. "We're no match, Hazel. I'm a businesswoman, he's a cowboy. At one point he even suggested I run Milady up in Mystery. Have you ever heard of anything so ridiculous?"

"In my time, I've heard better than that. And what's so impossible about living up here?" The cattle baroness frowned.

"It's wonderful here. But all I've got in my entire life is that business, and I'm not going to risk it any more than I already have, just to hang around town and moon after a cowboy who has his pick of women in Mystery—now that he's decided to get back in the saddle." Lyndie shook her head.

Hazel snorted. "I told you—a good man, a good snowstorm and a good bottle of wine is all you kids need—"

"We tried that last night. Trust me. And he didn't even have the grace to say goodbye." Lyndie adjusted her seat and swallowed the unshed tears in her throat. "I'm leaving, Hazel. It was a lovely experiment, but now it's over and I pronounce it a complete failure."

Hazel didn't seem to know what to say. She was silent for the rest of the ride to the airport. When she hugged Lyndie at the gate, she said, "Have more wishbone, darling. Sometimes life hands you cowboys when you want businessmen. That's just how it is.''

Lyndie grabbed her carry-on and gave her great-aunt a sad smile. "I don't want either. I just want to pay you back, and get on with my life at Milady." She kissed her, then walked onto the plane.

The plane ride back to New Orleans had been the longest trip Lyndie had ever taken. Crying in public was certainly not her thing, so she wiped her tears in every rest room, and with every transfer, she hardened her heart.

It was better this way, she'd told herself then—and now, almost a month later. She had no business even thinking of a life with Bruce Everett. They'd proven to be oil and water. She still laughed at the idea of her living in a two-room cabin in the back of Mystery Dude Ranch.

Unfortunately, that was how love was. For every cold chuckle she got from thinking of living in pen-ury in Mystery, she felt a deep bitter longing that all the mansions in the world couldn't fill. And even if she was willing to live in a small cabin with Bruce, the final death knell of their relationship had been when he didn't even say goodbye. He didn't love her. Men who loved ran after their girl at train stations. She'd seen it in the movies.

Well, he knew good and well where the Mystery Valley Airport was. And he hadn't showed up.

So that was that, she told herself, nibbling crackers at her desk in the back of the French Quarter shop, mulling over finances. Again.

She swore the pressure of paying Hazel back wasn't giving her headaches, it was making her positively nauseated.

When the phone rang, she almost jumped, she was so deep into her thoughts.

"All for Milady," she said perfunctorily.

"Darling? Is that my best grand-niece? You sure sound tuckered out!"

Lyndie smiled at Hazel's familiar voice. "Hazel! How goes it in Mystery? I've got a check for you. Half the loan. I'm about to overnight it this instant."

"A check?"

"You know darn well what that check's for— your MDR Corporation."

"Oh, that." Hazel acted as if she was trying to remember a two-dollar debt. "Well, don't bother yourself right now with that. I called to tell you that I want you to come up for the weekend. Just for us gals. The trees are changing color—you've never seen Mystery so beautiful."

Lyndie smiled into the receiver. "You know I wish I could, but I've got to get this loan paid off— and to tell you the truth, there's a certain man I don't want to see right now. I just couldn't take it."

"He's been such a nasty ill-tempered hermit in this valley, some woman either needs to shoot him or marry him."

"He's had plenty of chances," Lyndie replied, her heart twisting.

"The man had never quite grieved. When he rescued you, it took the choke-hold of guilt from him, and he was lost, not knowing where to go."

"I'll tell him where to go," Lyndie offered.

Hazel chuckled. "There are enough riled-up fillies here to do that, darling. But what I was saying is that he went back to his hibernating old ways as if to find himself. I was hoping—"

"I don't want to get involved. Sorry, Hazel. I love you dearly, but my heart and my body can only take so much before they're all scarred over and untouchable."

"Just for a quick weekend. We can do a little business—straighten out that loan—"

"Half's coming to you overnight."

"No! Darling, you're the most pigheaded McCallum I've ever known. Land sakes, you're worse than me! It's going to take a strong hand to tame you. Now listen, you can bring the payment up here if you like—"

Lyndie couldn't hide her sigh. "I can't, Hazel. Truly. If it was just the money, I might, but in truth, I haven't been feeling so well this week. I just couldn't fly right now."

"Oh." Hazel seemed undone, as if this was something she hadn't planned on.

"So, how 'bout I send that check?" Lyndie wanted to get back to the subject of business about which she was comfortable, and leave the subject of Bruce Everett far away.

"Don't send anything. I may just have to come down there for a visit, instead. Love you, darling. I'll call you when I know my plans."

Hazel's quick goodbye was puzzling, but Lyndie couldn't ponder it because the phone on her desk rang again.

She picked up the receiver.

"Hi, Dr. Feldman. This is Lyndie."

Lyndie's pleasant greet-the-public smile slowly died on her face. The sting in her eyes could only mean the onset of tears.

"Well, thanks for c-calling—" she stammered. "I-I'm sure after the disbelief wears off I'll be thrilled."

She placed the phone back on the receiver. Shocked, she found herself staring out from her office into the shop. Through the half-open door, her image stared back in the shop mirror, and with a hurt that was like a knife through her heart, she realized how the frilly lingerie that surrounded her was all wrong for the moment—or cruelly right. She didn't need black lace garters and pink padded bras.

No, mothers-to-be needed nursery rhymes and cash-mere booties.

The realization hit like a hurricane, devastating her, laying her emotionally flat. She was going to have a baby. There was no doubt. And also of no doubt, it was Bruce's baby.

The thought sent hot tears streaming down her face with no end to their supply. Now, no matter how painful, no matter how she prayed for closure, Bruce Everett was destined never to be gone from her life. Unlike Mitch who she'd been able to excise with an accountant and a lawyer, Bruce and her love for him was to remain, in the face of her baby, for-ever.

Lyndie put her face in her hands and sobbed. The call from the doctor had utterly broadsided her. She figured she had a flu or a gastrointestinal infection, but her nausea was from morning sickness.

She was pregnant.

Slowly, she dropped her head on the pile of pa-pers on her desk. She recalled time and time again how they'd made love with no protection. Now, she was paying the consequences for her impetuousness. She'd never pictured herself a single mother, but that was what she was going to be if Bruce chose not to participate in the rearing of their child.

The next step was to go to Montana. She would have to see him. Even she wasn't so cold as to tell him over the phone.

But she didn't know how she could bear seeing him. Weeks had passed since she'd seen or heard from him. He might have a steady girlfriend by now—someone who was the salt of the earth, a real Montana cowgirl who was perfect for him.

Now Lyndie and her news was going to throw a wrench in his life. But she would have to prepare herself for all the terrible possibilities, even though all of them bit into her heart hard.

"Honey, you okay?" asked Vera, her shopkeeper, when she came to the back to look for stock.

Lyndie raised her head. She wiped her tear-soaked cheeks. She didn't know how she was going to manage, but she knew she wanted this baby, wanted it like she wanted the father, and if she only got one of them, she was going to cherish him or her as no other.

"I'm fine, Vera. Fine. But look, I just found out I've got to go out of town. Do you think you can manage the shop while I'm gone?" She sniffed and patted her red eyes dry.

"I've been doing it fine for years. I'll manage. Maybe you need another vacation, huh?" Vera studied her, obviously not buying her story at all. "That last one took more out of you than it put back from the way you looked coming off that plane."

Lyndie stood at the door and took a good long look at her shop.

Several customers were inspecting the rows of

silk bras that had just come in for autumn in rich spice colors. A peignoir of palest ivory hung in the window, its sheer silk chiffon something that would add confection to a woman, not coverage.

"Can you get the peignoir out of the window for me, Vera. I'm going to take it with me. Put the flannels there, instead—you know, the black ones with the pink poodles. That'll be fun for a fall display."

"Sure. Right away." Vera gave her a strange look.

Lyndie had never taken anything from the shop but what was serviceable, but things were different now. *She* was different now. She was going to be a mother and she had the fight of her life yet to come. Her broken heart aside, she had to tell Bruce the aching truth. The rest would just be holding her breath. If they could work things out, she would be forever grateful. But if not, well, she would go down fighting—for herself, her baby and for the man she loved.

So, she was heading back to Montana.

Twelve

The next day, still tired and nibbling crackers, Lyndie checked the new shop she'd just opened in the Garden District.

Her plane ticket was purchased for a night flight to Denver. There she would stay overnight, then fly to Mystery in the morning. She just had to call Hazel with the unexpected news that she was coming up, after all.

But still, she hadn't picked up the phone. She couldn't bear the questions. Particularly those best answered face-to-face.

From the large glass window in front of the shop, she watched the live oaks scatter what few leaves they would lose in the fall. A breeze whisked away the last of the hot, sticky weather.

Her thoughts drifted north. She wondered what Mystery Valley looked like in a mantle of autumn, a chill to the air that whispered of snow and snuggling by the fireplace.

"So, how long you gonna be gone this time? Man, I should be the boss," Annie lamented, having just been promoted to the managerial position of the new store.

"Oh, it's hell being the boss. Truly." Lyndie gave her a wry smile. "You think I take a lot of vacation time, but the fact is, I'm never on vacation. I'm working all the time, in my head, and it's awful."

"So you say," Annie retorted good-naturedly.

Lyndie laughed. She was grateful for her loyal employees like Annie. Those that had been there for over five years were jewels, and she was bound and determined to treat them as such.

Besides, she was now looking out for two, and suddenly everything meant a lot to her.

"I just have to go over a few of the orders, then I'll cab it to the airport. I hope only to be gone a couple of days." She rubbed her flat belly almost subconsciously.

"Let me know if you need anything." Annie went to greet a woman who had just entered the shop.

Lyndie wasn't in the back room for more than fifteen minutes when Annie came sauntering in.

"We've had a lot of men looking for gifts at Milady, but I swear, none of them can hold a candle to the handsome creature who just came in."

"Good. Make him flirt with you, then he'll spend even more money, just to relieve the guilt of flirting with the shop girl." Lyndie gave a diabolical chuckle.

"He wants to see a bra and panty set in palomino. You ever heard of that color? I didn't want to look dense."

Lyndie stared at her. The word *palomino* made her think of Girlie. She wondered how the mare was getting on these days.

"Palomino is kind of a beigy-blond color." Lyndie furrowed her brow. "You know, I think we have a set in that color in the New York shipment. I'll bring them out for the display before I leave."

"Thanks." Annie raised her eyebrows. "Let me get back. I don't want him to leave without my phone number."

Lyndie shook her head, then she went into the storeroom to look for the box.

She found the set she was looking for. Taking an armful, she walked into the shop and placed the stack on the Victorian display case.

"I think this is pretty close to the color of a palomino. What size does your girlfriend wear?" Lyndie asked the man whose back was to her, as he looked at a silk camisole Annie held out in her hands.

He turned.

Lyndie's heart stopped.

She should have recognized the black cowboy hat, but in the South, sometimes men wore hats just like it.

Then again, she should have noticed the broad back, the tall stature. She should have known it was Bruce Everett just by the scent and the crackle of sexual tension in the air.

"Hello." Lyndie put down the bra and panty set she was about to hang up.

"Hello, Lyndie," Bruce said, his gaze strangely warm.

Annie's eyes popped out of her sockets.

When she realized Lyndie knew the hunk, she made a quick excuse to check the storeroom and left them alone.

"What brings you all the way down here?" Lyndie asked, caution in her voice.

"You. I came to see you. To tell you—" He hesitated. His expression became taut.

She hadn't realized how much she'd missed his hard, inscrutable face until now.

"To tell me what?" she asked solemnly.

"To tell you how good it feels to be released from Katherine. To tell you how great it feels to wipe the slate clean and be free. It took saving you on that mountain to make the ghosts disappear.''

His words strangely disappointed her.

"You could have written me a note. You didn't have to fly all the way down here,'' she admonished. "After all, you could have saved anyone up there on the mountain, it didn't have to be me.''

"But it was you.''

She glanced around the shop, trying to retain her detached attitude. "How did you know where my shop was?'' she ventured.

"Hazel told me.''

She nodded. "So that's why she called yesterday. On your behalf.''

He released a dismissive grunt. "I haven't seen Hazel since the Mystery Dude Ranch closed for the season. In fact, I only just talked to her this morning over the phone.''

His words didn't quite make sense to her, but she was through with making sense out of love.

"Strange. I was leaving to see Hazel this afternoon. She called and insisted I come up there for a few days. I figured it was on your account.''

"I can take care of my own business—just like you told me you could take care of yours, remember?''

She didn't reply. The tilt of her eyebrow was her only response.

He seemed thoroughly annoyed.

"What I came to say is that I'm sorry things got so out of hand," he began. "I didn't realize how crippled I was inside over Katherine until you came along. It was my responsibility to take you to the airport, and I found I just couldn't. After that time on the mountain, there was nothing left in me. I just had to sort it all out."

The wound inside her ripped open. He was saying he didn't love her, and for some strange reason, he felt the need to tell her personally.

The timing couldn't have been more cruel.

"Again," she stated, "you could have put this in a letter. You needn't have felt the obligation to come all the way here to tell me this personally."

"I wanted you to know."

It was her turn to grow annoyed. "Well, consider the message sent. I never once felt you shirked your duties. Hazel would have driven me to the airport whether you were around or not, so no problem." She studied him, still puzzled over his appearance at her shop.

His frustration seemed to grow. "What I want to say is, I'm sorry. I'm sorry I got you all involved with me and Katherine. I'm sorry for—well, for everything."

It seemed too horrible to have to suffer the same rejection over and over again, but somehow, that was what had come to pass. He was sorry he'd gotten involved with her, sorry he'd made love to her, sorry he'd dangled her along while he wrangled with Katherine's ghost.

She wanted to laugh and cry at the same time.

Certainly, the time to tell him about their child had now come and gone. He was making it brutally obvious he didn't want her, so there was no need to mention a child and throw a noose around his neck.

A marriage to a man she loved when there was no love in return was beyond her worse nightmare.

"Well, I'm glad you got that off your chest. And believe me, I don't lay in bed pining for you. I chalk up our time together as a lust thing, and that's all."

She swore she saw hurt on his face, but she didn't dare hope. The pain inside her was too raw and exposed at this point to ask anymore questions she didn't want to have answered.

The coldness in his eyes returned. His jaw tightened. "I'm glad it hasn't inconvenienced you."

Staring at him, she could barely get out the words. "I'm fine. Really. Only, I have a plane to catch. Hazel awaits."

He stepped aside to let her pass. She grabbed her overnight roll-aboard and her briefcase with her laptop. After saying farewell to Annie, she left to catch her waiting cab.

He watched until she was out of sight.

She slumped down in the cab, everything inside her crushed at the goodbye. Everything except her feelings for Bruce's child.

If she couldn't have love, then she vowed to make do with love's child.

Instead of calling Hazel, Lyndie decided to rent a car and surprise her, if that was possible given her grim mood.

She pulled the white sedan through the gates of the Lazy M around five in the evening the following day. Hazel's Caddy was right in front of the house, in the circular drive.

At least she's home, Lyndie thought, parking the rental behind Hazel's car.

"Land sakes, are my eyes deceiving me?" Ebby exclaimed when she opened the door.

Hazel looked up from the papers at her desk in the library. Lyndie spied her through the walnut pocket doors, her leopard reading glasses perched on her nose.

"The devil?" Hazel rose and went to Lyndie.

They hugged. And Lyndie could see the concern on Hazel's face. She might fool Bruce, but there was no lying to the cattle baroness.

"So, what is it?" she asked.

Lyndie broke from her, shaking her head. "I kind of needed a break. I'll tell you when things quiet down a bit. You mind if I go to my room and rest for a while?"

Hazel seemed to understand. She told Ebby to

send a tray to the guest room, then went with Lyndie to settle her in.

Unpacking her case, she finally was able to say, "Bruce came down to see me in New Orleans. In fact, I was on my way out the door to the airport when he stopped by the shop. I suppose he must have had a cowboy convention to go to down there, because what he had to say to me wasn't worth the trip."

"What did he say?" Hazel asked, as usual getting right to the point.

"He thanked me for helping him get over Katherine." Lyndie shrugged. She was amazed at how hard and cold she was becoming inside. She didn't feel like crying at all now; her tears had all frozen up.

"He loves you, Lyndie. I've never seen two people so right for each other. He wasn't down there for no convention. He'd come to see you," Hazel informed her.

"Do you know that for sure? He told you that?"

Hazel hesitated. "Well, truth to tell, I haven't talked to him much since you left. He holed himself up at the ranch and there was no dealing with him. The ranch hands said he was mean as a grizzly. He called yesterday to ask where your shop was, and I told him, figuring he was going to send you some flowers or something."

"Okay, so you don't know if he loves me."

Lyndie put down the pile of sweaters she'd gotten out of her suitcase. "But I think he made our relationship crystal clear when he apologized for everything. *Everything* is the word he used, and that pretty much says it all."

"You darn young folk! Neither of you can talk worth a damn. When Bruce gets back here, I'm gonna get the truth out of him or—"

"No." Lyndie was firm. Her conviction silenced Hazel. "It's really important that he not be coerced, Hazel. I don't need a man so badly that I've got to get him to the altar by putting a gun to his head, and—" she paused, choosing her words carefully "—and I think love is what makes a marriage work, and you can't force that."

Hazel hesitated. For there was nothing to refute the truth of Lyndie's words.

"He's gonna come here to see you. You know that, don't you?" the cattle baroness finally said.

"Let him. There's no reason why we shouldn't be friends."

The word *friend* got her cold ball of tears melting. She so desperately didn't want to be friends with Bruce; she wanted to be his partner, his lover, his wife, the mother of his children. The last thing she wanted was to be friends.

"I'll send in a tray of my homemade stew. Darling, you don't look too well, and I want you to rest.'' Hazel hugged her. "I may be a fool old woman, but I'm not giving up.''

"I can't have you interfering, Hazel." Lyndie held her gaze. "It's that important, okay?''

"I won't do a thing." Hazel held up her hands.

Lyndie shoved the sweaters aside and laid down on the bed. Suddenly she was exhausted.

Hazel gave her a worried frown. "I have to tell you, darling, that Bruce Everett's a man who gets what he wants. If he decides it's you, you'll have to surrender.''

Lyndie just closed her eyes. "If I'm what he wants, he's doing a poor job of showing me.''

A day later, Hazel rolled her Caddy along the rock-strewn road to the mill. Just as she thought, she found the lone male figure standing by the wheel, watching the water pour from the baskets.

Bruce looked up at the sound of the car.

Hazel took no time for warm-ups. She got out of her car, slammed the door and strode over to him.

"Somehow, I think this has to do with your grand-niece," he quipped, his eyes on the cattle baroness.

"Damn right," Hazel cursed. "What did you do to her?''

"I've done nothing except give her money for the business, watch her day and night, force her to stay at the ranch when all she wanted was to go home.

She used me like a bronc at a rodeo, and now you're asking me what I did to *her?*''

His disbelief was genuine, Hazel could tell.

She was caught off guard. "Your MDR Corporation made a good investment in All for Milady," she began.

"And she still thinks it was you who gave her the money?"

Hazel nodded.

"And she thinks you own Mystery Dude Ranch, and I'm nothing but a poor cowhand. And now how do I go about telling her the truth without thinking for the rest of my life that she married me for my financial assets and not the feeling in my heart?"

The older woman's groan was audible. "This is a fine mess. I've never seen a worse stalemate. She made me promise to not interfere, so I can't just lock you both up in a cabin until you both admit you love each other."

"She told me our relationship was 'just a lust thing.' I don't know if she could ever love me." He picked up a rock and skipped it across the tumbling waters.

"Well, I told her I won't interfere, and I won't." Hazel's blue eyes narrowed. "But I'm telling you this, take it for what it is. You both need to find out what's in your hearts, and leave the world and finances out of it.

"The best thing you could do would be to spirit

her away, take her to your daddy's stone hunting lodge up on Mystery Mountain, and don't let her leave until you both have an understandin'.''

Hazel made to leave. "Now that's all I'm sayin', you hear me? I'm not interfering, and if she asks if that was my idea, I plan on denying it. You're a man I'd be proud to have in the McCallum family, son, and yet, you got to be like a McCallum and just go after what you want.''

Bruce looked at her steadily.

Hazel drove away, breathless at the thought of the resolve she'd seen in his eyes.

The horse trailer pulled up to the ranch house at about eight o'clock the next morning.

When Lyndie arose, she looked outside at the ruckus. There was Girlie, all tacked up and ready to go, Beastie Boy right beside her.

"What?" she whispered, tying her flannel robe tightly around her waist.

"I think he's gone mad," Ebby said, her gaze glued to the parlor window.

"What's he up to?" Lyndie asked.

"He says you're going riding with him as soon as you're awake. Hazel didn't tell me anything about this.''

"Where is Hazel?" Lyndie fumed, her instincts telling her that her great-aunt was all over this idea.

"She went to Billings for a cattle show. Said if

the weather got bad, she won't be back till tomorrow.''

Lyndie heard the front door thrown open and the sound of cowboy boots on polished oak floors. She turned to the parlor entrance. Bruce stood there, an impatient expression on his face.

"You up?" he asked.

She nodded.

"Then, get dressed. We got a two-hour ride up the mountain."

"I never agreed to this. I told Hazel—"

"The old gal's got nothing to do with it. I'm here doing it, and I say we're going up the mountain."

She wanted to stay and bicker with him, but she just didn't have the energy. Instead, she went with Ebby to get dressed and suck down a cup of tea and some biscuits.

"Ready?" He smiled as she strode through the hall toward him. The wolf was back.

"I don't recall being asked about this. You know, if you're forcing me to go with you, technically that's kidnapping, and it's a federal charge." She raised one eyebrow at him.

He shrugged his broad shoulders and grinned. "Sure. I understand. And when we get back, if you want to call the feds and press charges, you can call from my phone. But now, let's go."

She followed him out the door and let him give her a leg up on Girlie. Before she knew it, they were past the Lazy M, heading north up Mystery Mountain.

There was a lot they could have talked about, but somehow, she didn't feel like talking. On this beautiful ride past shimmering golden aspens and mountain ponds glistening the blue of the sky, she was in no hurry to acquire another rejection. Instead, she let the peace of the landscape soothe her frazzled nerves.

One hour fed into another, until they came upon a small fieldstone cabin nestled deep in a ravine on Mystery Mountain. Smoke wafted from the chimney.

She didn't think they would stop, but Bruce immediately dismounted and held Girlie for her.

"So, what's this?" she asked, steadying herself. "You know these people?"

"My dad built this cabin. It was a place to go when he needed to think, or when he and my mom just wanted to get away from all their kids. They had a bunch, I think I told you."

"It's lovely," she remarked.

"Go on inside."

She hesitated, then opened the battened door. A fire crackled in the hearth; at the table was a bouquet of black-eyed susans stuffed into a coffee cup. No one was home.

Transfixed, she walked farther into the little room. In the corner was a pine bedstead with piles of hand-made quilts. Over the bed was a faded linen needle-point that said *Home is where the Heart is*.

"This cabin's mine now. Mom and Dad both died."

"I'm sorry," she said.

He stared at her. "Do you like it?"

"You live here?" she asked, amazed.

"The place has no electricity, no phone, nothing but comfort and the beauty of the landscape."

She softened. If he loved her, she'd live in the small cabin with him, no questions asked. But still, there had to be love.

"All right. I give up. What's this about?" she finally asked. "If Hazel's not orchestrating this, then you are, and what's the message?"

He went to her and slipped a strong hand around her waist.

She had to admit, his touch was like a drug, one which she hadn't known she was in withdrawal from, until now.

"I kidnapped you and brought you here so that maybe we could start over." His eyes were dark with apprehension. "I know you think what we had was only a 'lust thing,' as you called it, but it was more to me. The minute I saw you, I was drawn to you. I realized that I needed you in my life for so many reasons, and when you left for New Orleans, I realized I had to go get you and bring you back."

"Because why?" she asked, holding her breath.

"Because I love you. I want to marry you. I want to have a bunch of kids just like Mom and Dad. And I want to go to my grave loving one woman and one woman only."

She stared at him, wondering if she was dreaming. It didn't seem possible that all this was inside him and she had never known.

But somehow, she was awake and the words were clear as day.

"Do you think you could tolerate a life of me loving you, girl?" he whispered, his face hard with uncertainty.

She couldn't quite take it all in—he loved her.

She had been wrong about him; he wasn't just another man out to sexually conquer—he loved her.

Terrified, and yet desperately wanting, she stammered, "I n-never thought I could trust another man. After Mitch's betrayal…"

He pulled her to him and kissed her hair. "That's gone now, girl. It's a whole new world up here in Montana. A whole new world."

"He killed everything inside me. Everything. I never thought I would feel again."

"I know," he answered, brushing the hair from her tear-bright eyes.

She locked gazes with him. The eyes that had once seemed so steely and cold now held nothing but the warmth of love, and she believed him. "But I feel now. I feel everything again," she wept. "And you are the one who gave that to me. You. Only you."

"Then, you'll marry me?"

She laughed through her tears. "Yes. Yes. Yes," she repeated, the ice ball melting inside her, the tears flowing fast and furious. "I loved you when we made love in your tent. I knew then that I didn't want to return to New Orleans, that I could move Milady to Mystery if I wanted to, but I thought it was no use. If you didn't love me, there was no future here. And I couldn't tell how you were feeling—you'd gone so cold."

His mouth twisted in a wry frown. "Guilt is a terrible thing to have to wrangle with. I'm sorry. It took me a while to sort out what had happened between us and why. But when I knew, I knew."

He kissed her then, the kiss of a soul mate.

She felt him pull her to the rough pine bedstead. He sat and brought her to him, slowly, erotically unbuttoning her fleece shirt.

Her breath quickened. The longing inside her built, and she was so exquisitely happy to be alone and in love with him.

Sheepishly, she said, "Not to change the subject, but do you think we could put in electricity here, at least when the kids come along? You know that might be sooner than later..."

"Let's get started on that first baby right now."

Her hand went unconsciously to her still-flat

belly. "I have a shock for you, Mr. Everett. We're way ahead of the game."

He stopped, then stared at her as if she'd suddenly grown wings and turned into an angel. "True?" he gasped.

Fear fluttered inside her. But it was too late to back out now. "It's true. We've got way less than nine months to get to the chapel, but I never liked big drawn-out weddings, anyway. A short and sweet ceremony in front of the justice of the peace is fine with me. I hope this won't be a problem."

He tossed his head back and laughed.

"Darling, none of that's going to be a problem. Trust me."

And she did.

Thirteen

———

Hazel's cinnamon-and-black Fleetwood pulled into the Lazy M's drive late the next day. She hardly had time to get out of the car before Ebby ran out with the news.

"Bruce asked Lyndie to marry her. They're in town right now picking out the ring!"

The cattle baroness didn't bother to hide the "I knew it!" look on her handsome face. Her smile made her look ten years younger.

"They have to have the wedding here." Hazel placed her hands to her cheeks. "We've got to get busy! No sense in wasting time. They should tie the knot before Christmas. That way when the baby comes—"

"Baby!" Ebby looked close to fainting.

Hazel shrugged. "I don't know for sure, but I'd place a bet on it. So let's get going. It takes a lot to throw a wedding in just a few weeks. We've got to notify the minister, get a caterer, a tent…"

Just as Hazel finished, she turned to find Bruce's trusty old red diesel truck pulling into the ranch. Lyndie was sitting next to Bruce in the middle, as if they were already a married couple.

Hazel beamed a grin. "I heard the news!" she hollered. "And to think, this is the first match that I had nothing to do with!"

Bruce helped Lyndie out of the truck. Hazel grabbed her left hand and oohed over the perfect diamond solitaire that had been slipped on her ring finger.

"He spent too much, I think," Lyndie confessed. "I'm afraid we might need the money to put an addition on our cabin—for our, uh…little addition."

Bruce grinned. His smile told her it was all right with him.

"But first things first." Lyndie reached inside her purse. She took out an envelope.

"Before I get any more in debt, I want to pay you back for the loan you made."

She handed Hazel the envelope. "This is for MDR Corporation. It's half. I'll have the other half for you when I dissolve the stores down in New Orleans."

Hazel looked at the envelope. Then at Bruce.

Lyndie looked at both of them, confused.

Bruce put his arm around her. "Darling, I guess you'd better just hold on to that check. Hazel doesn't own MDR Corporation. I do."

Confused, Lyndie studied his expression, then turned to Hazel.

"He's right there, dear," Hazel confirmed. "MDR stands for Mystery Dude Ranch. He owns that, too, by the way."

"But I always thought you owned that," Lyndie exclaimed.

"You just always assumed I was behind everything. But it was Bruce, really, all along."

Squeezing his hand, Lyndie turned to him. "But if you have the ranch, why do you live in that tiny cabin up Mystery Mountain?"

He shook his head and dazzled her with an apologetic grin. "I told you my parents used that to get away from it all, and so do I. But, honey, I got an old ranch a hundred miles from here, with a ranch house big enough for ten children.

"I do the dude ranch in the summer just for fun. I monitor my cattle online. Which is how you're going to run your shops when you put your corporate headquarters up here."

Stunned, she finally said, "But you hardly knew me when MDR put up that money. Why would you take such a risk for a stranger?"

"From the minute I saw you I never felt you were a stranger."

He looked at Hazel.

The cattle baroness winked.

"I admit," he added, "I did have a little head start on getting to know you from your great-aunt."

"Yes, her and her wicked matchmaking ways," Lyndie accused.

"Not guilty!" Hazel objected, the grin still on her face.

"But when you arrived," Bruce continued, staring down at her, "I realized this was it. It was easy to invest. Hell, I even liked the name of your store."

"You mean All for Milady?" she asked.

"Yep," he answered, smiling, kissing her. "But I've got to confess, in my mind I call it 'All for My Lyndie.'"

The following week, the *Mystery Gazette* read:

Wealthy Montana cattleman Mr. Bruce Everett wed New Orleanian Ms. Melynda Clay, in a private ceremony at the ranch of the bride's great-aunt, Mrs. Hazel McCallum. The bride wore an antique blue satin gown. After a honeymoon steamboating down the Mississippi, the couple will reside in Mystery, which will be the new international headquarters for the bride's chain of lingerie stores, All For Milady.

Hazel read and reread the announcement as Ebby poured her an after-dinner glass of aged sherry.

"A happier husband, I don't think I've ever seen," Ebby commented.

The cattle baroness put down the paper and

reached for her sherry. "Let's toast another successful match in Montana."

Ebby poured herself a glass and clinked the fine crystal with Hazel. "So, does this mean you're finally going to retire from this matchmaking game?" she asked.

"Do I lose heifers in a whiteout?" Hazel's famed Prussian-blue eyes twinkled. "The McCallums always have to find new territory, Ebby. It's in our blood."

Ebby rolled her eyes and went to take her sherry to the kitchen to finish the dishes. "The west was settled a hundred years ago," she called back. "There is no new territory."

Hazel quipped to her departing back, "Not true, Ebby. The biggest territory lies ahead."

The housekeeper stopped. "And what territory is that?"

Hazel smiled to herself. "Why, it's love, of course."

* * * * *

*Don't miss the next
book in Meagan McKinney's*
MATCHED IN MONTANA *series!*
*Look for BILLIONAIRE BOSS, coming in
April 2003 from Silhouette Desire.*

Silhouette®

Desire®

USA TODAY bestselling author

CAIT LONDON

**brings you a captivating new series
featuring to-die-for alpha heroes
from the Pacific Northwest!**

HEARTBREAKERS

**He'll stir his woman's senses, and when
she's dizzy with passion...he'll propose!**

MR. TEMPTATION
(Silhouette Desire #1430)

Gorgeous widower Jarek Stepanov must release his guilt
about the past, open his heart and convince vulnerable
beauty Leigh Van Dolph that she belongs in his arms.

And the excitement continues in April 2003 with:

INSTINCTIVE MALE
(Silhouette Desire #1502)

Tough but vulnerable Ellie Lathrop unexpectedly finds
love with the one man who has always gotten under
her skin—Mikhail Stepanov.

Available at your favorite retail outlet.

Silhouette®

Where love comes alive™

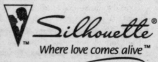

COMING NEXT MONTH

#1501 TAMING THE BEASTLY MD—Elizabeth Bevarly

Dynasties: The Barones

When nurse Rita Barone needed a date for a party, she asked the very intriguing Dr. Matthew Grayson. Things heated up, and Rita wound up in Matthew's bed, where he introduced her to sensual delight. However, the next morning they vowed to forget their night of passion. But Rita couldn't forget. Could she convince the good doctor she needed his loving touch—*forever?*

#1502 INSTINCTIVE MALE—Cait London

Heartbreakers

Desperate for help, Ellie Lathrop turned to the one man who'd always gotten under her skin—enigmatic Mikhail Stepanov. Mikhail ignited Ellie's long-hidden desires, and soon she surrendered to their powerful attraction. But proud Mikhail wouldn't accept less than her whole heart, and Ellie didn't know if she could give him that.

#1503 A BACHELOR AND A BABY—Marie Ferrarella

The Mom Squad

Because of a misunderstanding, Rick Masters had lost Joanna Prescott, the love of his life. But eight years later, Rick drove past Joanna's house—just in time to save her from a fire and deliver her baby. The old chemistry was still there, and Rick fell head over heels for Joanna and her baby. But Joanna feared being hurt again; could Rick prove his love was rock solid?

#1504 TYCOON FOR AUCTION—Katherine Garbera

When Corrine Martin won sexy businessman Rand Pearson at a bachelor auction, she decided he would make the perfect corporate boyfriend. Their arrangement consisted of three dates. But Corrine found pleasure and comfort in Rand's embrace, and she found herself in unanticipated danger—of surrendering to love!

#1505 BILLIONAIRE BOSS—Meagan McKinney

Matched in Montana

He had hired her to be his assistant, but when wealthy Seth Morgan came face-to-face with beguiling beauty Kirsten Meadows, he knew he wanted to be more than just her boss. Soon he was fighting to persuade wary Kirsten to yield to him—one sizzling kiss at a time!

#1506 WARRIOR IN HER BED—Cathleen Galitz

Annie Wainwright had gone to Wyoming seeking healing, not romance. Then Johnny Lonebear stormed into her life, refusing to be ignored. Throwing caution to the wind, Annie embarked on a summer fling with Johnny that grew into something much deeper. But what would happen once Johnny learned she was carrying his child?